MATILDA HART

SECRETS & FRESH BEGINNINGS

AF354029

Secrets & Fresh Beginnings
Matilda Hart
Copyright © 2023
Cover design by Mats Ingelborn with images by
Prostooleh, Starline and Freepik.
Author's portrait by Mego Studio
ISBN print: 978-91-89822-01-6
ISBN e-book: 978-91-89822-00-9
Published by Yabot AB, Sweden, 2023

Pierre looked into the child's eyes and knew it would soon die. He could see the life draining out of the child's gaze like sand slipping through an hourglass, and he knew there was not a thing he could do to stop it. Its time had come, and there was nothing he could do. A coldness gripped his heart.

"I actually think she looks better," said the mother, stroking the little girl over the hair. "Don't you agree, doctor? Her cheeks have more color? She was so pale when she came home from the hospital, but now…"

Her voice trembled, and she looked pleadingly at him despite knowing that her little daughter would die. There was nothing medical science could do. He had told her so before the girl was released from the hospital.

Somewhere inside her black curly head, in the cerebellum, there was a tumor barely larger than a pinhead. He had discovered it by pure chance, it was almost invisible on the X-rays, but it was there. He knew it was there. His two colleagues at the Saint Orbona hospital had confirmed its existence. But there was nothing they could do.

The little tumor was too deeply encased in that vital organ, and they could not access it. They were specialists. They had studied with the best in the USA and abroad. They had the best technical resources at their disposal and saved many lives where other doctors had stood powerless. But in this case, they managed nothing, and Mrs. Landry knew it as well as he did. But she didn't want to realize that her girl would die; she clung to the last straw called hope. She clung to the hope that a faint color on the girl's cheeks from the first sun rays of spring over Washington D.C., that she still played in the yard, oblivious and without sadness, that she continued to laugh and chatter as usual. As any typical five-year-old would. The mother couldn't see the signs in the girl's large sparkling brown eyes or the slight tense, stiff movements that indicated approaching ataxia.

"Well, Mrs. Landry," he said slowly, "she actually looks better. The sun will be stronger in a few weeks, and she can stay out longer and get even more color on her cheeks."

He released his gentle grip on the little one's chin and rose while the girl ran off to her corner of the big untidy room and started playing with a dollhouse. The Landrys lived in the less fortunate areas, on the outskirts of Washington D.C., in a trailer park just off the highway. But finding houses or apartments in good condition with such cheap rent was nearly impossible.

While washing off at the kitchen sink and drying his hands on the clean towel Mrs. Landry had laid out for him, he once again wondered about life's injustices. Why should some people be forced to live like this while others enjoyed a life in the sun and luxury? And he came to think of Clara, who was probably sipping a drink in Laurier's bar with her father while she waited for him to join them. She was the only daughter of one of the state's wealthiest men. She had studied law and proudly accepted a place as a paralegal at one of the city's prominent law firms. But she had spent her childhood and youth in a palace-like villa by Montrose Park and found it hard to understand and share his love for these poor people.

"You have no ambition, Pierre," she could say. "You have a solid education, and you have made a name for yourself as one of the best brain surgeons in the country…
… and then you bury your career in a place like Saint Orbona Hospital. The whole world could be open to you, if only …"

And he couldn't explain to her that he had already opened the gates to the world where he belonged and did not want anything else. He liked working at the hospital, which was funded by Catholic organizations. He loved the patients who almost invariably thought that a hundred dollars were a considerable sum as a fee for advanced brain surgery. He did not want to trade them for others who had wealth but lacked gratitude.

Mrs. Landry came and looked shyly up at him. She was a small thin woman who looked much older than her thirty years. In ten years, she would really look old.

"How much do we owe you, doctor?" She held a worn purse against her chest.

He smiled and shook his head.

"Nothing, Mrs. Landry. This was just a regular free check-up. I just wanted to see how little Freyja was doing." He put on his jacket. "You have to promise me to call as soon as something happens."

They looked at each other and could hear the girl singing to her doll in the other room.

"Will it be long?" Mrs. Landry formed the unspeakable question with pale, thin lips.

He shrugged.

"It is hard to say. You will notice that she will find it more difficult to walk and harder to see. Contact us as soon as it happens. We don't want her to suffer needlessly."

The woman's eyes filled with tears, but she nodded as a sign that she understood.

"You are so kind, Doctor Pierre," she murmured. "Without you, I don't know what we would have done."

His face hardened, and he suddenly looked more than the thirty-five years he was. *Without me, you would have had to do precisely the same thing. I have not been able to do you much,* was what he thought. But he said, "Enjoy her laughter, Mrs. Landry. Being able to laugh is the greatest remedy for the moment."

As he drove into downtown Washington DC, his thoughts drifted back to Clara. And he wondered why she had been so keen for him to meet her father.

He had known Clara for a few months. They had first met at his good friends' Peter and Astrid Dahl. He had seen her over the edge of his cocktail glass as she entered the room—tall, slim, and blonde with an almost perfectly modeled face, exquisitely dressed, and with a confident gait. He had immediately been interested in Clara Busch. His life had almost exclusively consisted of work, and there had been very little time for romance.

The interest was mutual.

Clara naturally knew who he was: Pierre Lyon-Cote, the young renowned neurosurgeon, included on the list of the most eligible bachelors by the Washington City Paper: above average height, slim but well built, thick black hair, brown eyes, and with a nose that was too big but gave character to the kind, open face.

He instinctively knew she was a rare beauty and an attractive woman. Astrid Dahl had volunteered the not-so-obvious information: Clara was twenty-four years old, a paralegal at the Department of Justice, and the daughter of Eric G. Busch, the successful industrial businessman.

Two days later, they had dinner at a popular tavern overlooking the river at The Wharf. That night Clara became part of Pierre's life. He had spoken of marriage the first week, but she had always shrugged it off with a laugh.

"I could never imagine living outside D.C.," she said. "It may border our country's capital, but it's just glorified farmland. You must have something better to offer me, P." And that's when he realized she would never be satisfied with a medical doctor devoting his time to underprivileged patients at Saint Orbona Hospital, where he would never get the income she apparently demanded.

The thought had made him uneasy, but he was still very fond of her. Maybe she would eventually appreciate his life and profession, and he did not lose hope. But he felt like he did as Mrs. Landry: clinging to a hopeless illusion.

Now he was on his way to the first meeting with Clara's father, and he had no idea why she had arranged it.

Traffic around Senate Park was as busy as always. It was in the late hours of the afternoon. The normal flow of tourist coaches, delivery vans, and taxis was mixed with cars and people hurrying from their jobs to catch a round of golf before the pale spring sun disappeared. The shadows were already long over the official buildings and the monuments. It was only the beginning of April, and it had been an unusually cold beginning of the year so far; only the bravest plants had pushed up their buds in the parks.

He parked his car in the parking reserved for guests at Laurier's.

Pierre Lyon-Cote turned up his collar. He shivered at the thought of the upcoming meeting. He suddenly wished Clara was just one of those everyday office girls walking down from the office to the shopping mall instead of the daughter of one of the state's wealthiest men.

With an uneasy feeling, he walked toward the restaurant's entrance. Every time he came here, he felt small in front of this old and pompous establishment with its prominent list of famous guests.

As he pulled open the door, a lithe fair-haired boy came rushing out and flew like an arrow across the path toward the busy street. Someone called out, but the boy did not listen. He was already by the lane of taxis waiting outside.

Pierre turned around, and with a few long steps, he ran after the boy and caught him by the collar just as the little one was about to throw himself into the constant stream of cars. The boy turned up two large blue eyes full of disappointment at him.

”Easy, kid! Are you thinking of killing yourself?”

The boy tried to pull away, but in the same instant, a calm, clear voice was heard:

”Listen to the man, Anders! He just wants to keep you safe.”

Pierre turned around without letting go of the boy and met one of the most beautiful women he’d ever seen. She was tall, only inches shorter than him. She wore a figure-hugging green dress, emphasizing her well-built body and soft female lines. Her shoulder-length curly hair shone as copper, but it was her face that made him gasp. There wasn’t a single feature about it that was wrong, and it was still full of life: the lips soft and red, the wings of her nose trembled with excitement, and the big green eyes that looked at him with gratitude and great relief.

She said something to the boy and took his hand, then smiled with strong white teeth at Pierre.

”I’m so sorry ... but Anders is really excited today. Thank you for intervening. I am Lise Norrgard. We are on our way to pick up my husband at the airport. He has worked in Europe for a few weeks, and Anders loves his father. Lunch was ...” She shrugged. ”He kept nagging about being too late.” She smiled. ”I’m so grateful. Sometimes one should have eyes in the back of one’s neck when you have a son as Anders.”

He finally managed to take his eyes off her. He didn’t understand why he felt so excited about the sight of her, but somehow it was as if he had known her forever.

Maybe it was her Scandinavian appearance or just because she was so strikingly beautiful.

"I guess it is better to have four eyes when watching a child" he murmured.

"Yes, and that's why I'm so delighted my husband is finally back. Anders can be difficult at times."

For a moment, they stood looking at each other. The traffic noise isolated them and made them feel alone on an island. Then she smiled and looked at her watch.

"I guess I have to go on then," she said, taking his hand. "Thank you, once again."

Her hand was firm and soft, and his palm felt empty as she pulled away and walked to a taxi with Anders tugging at his mother's arm.

Pierre stood and watched as the taxi disappeared, swallowed by the traffic. He felt bewildered and overwhelmed by the brief encounter. Pulling together and walking back toward the restaurant, he realized he had not introduced himself. She must think he was such a hick.

Somehow it hurt to think that he left that impression on this woman—a woman he would probably never see again.

"Pierre, you are late! Hurry up! Dad is waiting upstairs." Clara jumped down from the high stool. Her beautiful face with the large blue eyes did not bother to hide her irritation.

"You can get a drink up there…but I don't think you deserve one."

Eric G. Busch had reserved a private dining room on the second floor for his first meeting with the young doctor Clara wanted to introduce. He had done this to impress Pierre, but as he stood before the tall young man with intelligent brown eyes, he understood that that was done in vain. This man was not impressed by material things and exclusive surroundings. Busch felt a wave of displeasure. Clara had obviously chosen a man of character and integrity, but he now wondered if Pierre would accept his proposal. He hated disappointing his only daughter, and Clara would be furious if Pierre Lyon-Cote didn't accept.

They sat down at the large table set for three, and two waiters had been set aside to serve Mr. Busch and his guests in the best way possible.

Pierre listened to Clara and her father and answered in monosyllabic words while he enjoyed a cold beer. Busch had ordered a whisky for him, but Pierre declined as liquor was too strong if he was called back to the hospital. But after a while, he reconsidered as he needed something stronger; his mind was preoccupied. The meeting with the beautiful redhead and her son still tickled his nerves, and there was an underlying bitter sadness after the visit to the dying little girl, Freyja Landry.

Only when they had enjoyed the delicious three-course menu did he start to realize what Clara's father wanted.

"It has always been a dream of mine to do something for mankind," said Eric G. Busch, running his fingers through his short gray hair. "And now it looks like my dream will be realized. The DC Council has granted my plans, and the project has already started."

"Go on, Dad," Clara said, looking at her dad with intense appreciation. "Pierre won't believe it!"

Busch radiated ill-concealed pride. He was a man of indomitable power and keen intellect. Still, Pierre had a feeling something was missing with him.

"All right, I won't keep Pierre guessing. The thing is, I'm funding and building a new hospital, the most advanced in D.C. It is built on an old industrial plot with lovely views of the river. It will be a medical center with many clinical departments, and one will be the country's most advanced neurosurgery clinic. So I would like to ask you, Pierre, if you are interested in taking the clinic's leadership. Clara has recommended you highly, but I have, of course, also done my own research into your achievements, and you have gained a well-worth reputation."

His bright, almost gray eyes stared at Pierre, who sat silent and confused.

Busch had disclosed his dream. But he had also touched on Pierre's secret dream: working in an ultra-modern neurosurgical clinic and being able to implement new treatments that the Saint Orbona Hospital didn't have resources for.

"That...that sounds fantastic," he mumbled. "I am overwhelmed."

Clara's hand, slim and firm, caressed his hand with grace and love.

"Then you'll take it?" she exclaimed.

He looked at her. What had she expected? He met her gaze, her beautiful face, and found a hint of relief and fear. He wondered why she had been so worried that he wouldn't accept. Maybe it was more to her father's proposition...something that was not so easy to accept?

"The hospital will, of course, be open for all?" he said lightly, looking at Mr. Busch, whose face reddened.

"All details are not yet final," he answered with a tinge of uncertainty. "There will, of course, be an outpatient department, but the hospital is first and foremost intended for the politicians and foreign emissaries who can pay for the best treatments in the country."

Pierre sat motionless and silent, suddenly filled with a wave of unreasonable anger that he had difficulty controlling. It was always like this. The rich would have the first seat at the laid-out table, then if there were a few crumbs left, the rest could have their pick.

He looked at Clara and saw that she knew what he was feeling and that she did not like it.

With Mr. Busch, it was different. If he understood what Pierre was thinking, he did not let it show. His voice was still jovial and almost cheerful as he continued:

"Well, it's not a decision you have to make today. My offer stands for three months. If you accept, you are welcome; if not"— he shrugged—"then I am unfortunately forced to let someone else take it."

He called out to the waiter and asked for coffee. Cups, glasses, and steaming hot espressos were brought in as they withdrew to the lounge.

"How could you, Pierre!" Clara exclaimed furiously when they got to his two-bedroom apartment in Arlington Heights. It was not a very friendly neighborhood, and it was quite a drive from the hospital, but the rent was low, and he had a nice view over the park from the balcony.

"I don't understand how Dad could take it so lightly. You were downright rude to him!" She went to the kitchen and poured herself a glass of wine, then she sank into the couch and kicked off her shoes.

He didn't answer but turned on the tv instead. The news talked about violent protests in Seattle and the wildfires in California that were finally under control, but the main news report was about a passenger plane that had crashed on approach to Dulles airport. Instantly he wondered if Lise Norrgard's husband had been on that plane, but then he pushed away the thought. It was an absurd coincidence. Hundreds of planes landed at Dulles every day. Little Anders would surely meet his father again.

"You could at least have pretended to be interested," he heard Clara continue. "Dad made time for you. His time is incredibly valuable, and I am almost certain he came only to meet you."

"He gave me time to think," muttered Pierre and opened the doors to the balcony as if fresh air would clear the room of her anger.

A large flock of crows passed overhead, their calls drowning Clara's words. Her words returned as the birds settled in a tree in the park.

"... and I know him! He was unsure and annoyed with you, and Dad doesn't like people, which makes him insecure. My God, Pierre, this is a fantastic opportunity. Why didn't you accept without question?"

He turned and looked at her. She had emptied her glass, and he noticed she had poured one for him too. Suddenly he felt a strong need for alcohol. There was something he had to wash away. He took the glass and swallowed half in two large gulps, then looked almost sad at her.

"Do you really believe that money and success are the most important things in this life, Clara?" he said. "Doesn't such things as satisfaction with one's work and personal feelings mean something?"

"Your work would become more important at Dad's hospital than at this cheap…at Saint Orbona! As for your personal feelings, it cannot be the worst thing to work at one of our country's best hospitals, as head of your own clinic? What are you now? You are just an aid for Peter Dahl and Dr. Austen. They dump everything on you that they don't want!"

He wanted to explain to her that she didn't understand. They did so because they instinctively knew that he would treat these cases better than they would even if they had the same education. To be a brain surgeon was to look beyond rank and see what really was required… something few professionals were capable of. He was fortunate to have colleagues that looked at the patient's needs first and disregarded status and prestige.

He knew that he was the best doctor for these cases, and he did so without thoughts of his career, and he never lied—not even to himself.

"For me, helping people is the most important thing, Clara," he said softly as if speaking to a child. "And I would never be happy at a hospital built for the wealthy."

"They need you as much as the others!"

"Maybe so, but the others can't afford the fees for my services. Therefore I have to stay with them."

She stared at him in dismay.

"You...you are going to decline Dad's offer!" she exclaimed harshly.

He didn't have time to answer as his cell phone interrupted with its intense tone. He answered automatically. She saw his face become rigid and watchful, she heard him ask a few short, direct questions, and finally, she heard him say what she dreaded most:

"Get ready for surgery, sister Elena. I'm coming!"

He had hung up and dialed a number, then he hung up again.

"Unfortunately, I have to go to the hospital, Clara. An emergency has come in, and I have to operate."

"But you have the evening off. Didn't you say it was Peter's evening?"

"Peter is at home with a fever, the flu. And Austen is at a conference in New York."

"But..." She got up and ran to him on her stocking feet. She threw her arms around his neck and looked at him, almost pleading. "You can't go now. We have so much to talk about. We have to come to a decision."

"I have to, Clara! It's a matter of life or death. Don't you understand that?"

"You cannot drive, you have been drinking."

"I called for a taxi, but there was a twenty-minute wait. I haven't had so much that I can't drive."

He went into the bedroom to get ready, and when he returned, she was standing by the balcony.

"Will you be here when I get back?" he asked.

"I don't know," she said softly.

For a moment, he thought about walking up to her, but then he changed his mind. Shrugging his shoulders, he walked towards the door.

"If you get hungry, Mrs. Tangen has surely stocked up the refrigerator when she cleaned this morning."

Clara didn't answer, and he couldn't wait. A ten-year-old girl's life was hanging by a thread after a fall from a third-floor balcony.

He decided to take the longer, but probably faster, George Washington Memorial Parkway. The sun had set, and he was alert as he drove through the dark park. The highway lay almost empty before him as if the capital of the USA had been emptied of people.

It was when he had passed the river on Memorial Bridge that it happened.

A shadow appeared out of the darkness from a shrubbery, and Pierre saw it too late.

He stepped on the brake so that the car skidded and came to a stop against the curb; despite his fast reaction, something was thrown over the hood with a heart-stopping noise, and the shadow was nowhere to be seen.

For a moment, he sat motionless, his hands exhausted as the fingers clutched hard at the steering wheel. He opened the door and stepped out. Cold sweat broke out on his forehead when he saw what had happened.

There was a man on the tarmac, just in front of the right wheel.

He was dressed in a worn coat and lay motionless on his back. His staring eyes glistened in the pale moonlight when Pierre bent down to feel for the pulse, he felt none.

The man was dead.

He must have died instantly on impact with the car.

Pierre straightened up and heard his own heavy breathing. He wiped his face with a handkerchief and looked around. No eyewitnesses or frightened people had stopped to look at the accident. The few cars on the four-lane highway just passed, minding their own business.

He took another look at the dead man, unlocked his cell, and called 911.

"I have hit a man on the Interstate. He is…" He got no further. He couldn't bring himself to say that the man was dead. Something locked inside him.

"I am sending an ambulance," the operator responded calmly, "and the police. Please stay where you are, sir."

Pierre turned and walked slowly around the car as if in a trance. Was it his fault? His fault…his fault…?

He didn't know. He had no idea what had happened. Everything had happened so fast. At one moment, the road was empty and deserted; the next, the unknown man stumbled out in front of his car.

He dialed another number:

"Hello, Elena, it is Doctor Pierre. I will be late…there's been an accident…"

It did not take long before blue lights flashed over the road and the whole scene, and the man was lifted into the ambulance.

”To the hospital?” said one of the men in the ambulance, looking at a policeman. The policeman that seemed to come straight from the academy, looked around for help.

”There is no point. He is dead,” helped Pierre. ”I am a doctor. Take him to the morgue!”

The ambulance drove off. Another policeman, a big burly man with a grumpy face, turned to Pierre.

”You say you’re a doctor?”

”Yes, I’m Dr. Pierre Lyon-Cote, and work at Saint Orbona Hospital. I don’t know how this happened…”

”Let’s investigate that further when we talk at the station. We need to write a report, and we can write a report…”

”I can’t!” interrupted Pierre.

”Can’t?” The policeman said sharply with raised eyebrows.

Pierre shook his head.

”No, I have to go to the hospital. I was on my way when the accident happened. I have an emergency—the girl’s life depends on me.”

He turned to his old car; it didn’t seem damaged by the accident.

”I have to go now; I can come down to the station later for your report.”

One policeman motioned to prevent him from getting into the car, but the big one lowered his arm.

"Easy, Ben. The doctor is right. His surgery must come first. We'll do the interview later but we need a breathalyzer test right now."

Pierre blew long and hard and watched the policeman as he looked at the result. When he turned his gaze to Pierre, he looked almost threatening.

"It's close to the limit. Let's go, but no tricks, doctor. This accident must be investigated. You don't run over a person and kill him without questions."

Pierre said nothing. He just stared emptily at the policeman's sullen face, then moved to his car.

"No, doctor. We'll drive you. Get in the back seat."

They drove him to the hospital without further conversation, and all he thought about was the policeman's words: You don't run over a person and kill him without questions.

What did he mean?

What did he think?

It was all an accident. He had not been careless. The stranger had come out of nowhere.

Didn't the cops believe that?

Or did they have a different idea?

The feeling of creeping, approaching danger did not go away, not even during the hours in the operating theater, and he could not understand how he succeeded with the surgery.

It wasn't very complicated, but it was difficult enough. The ten-year-old girl had a cracked skull from the fall from the balcony, and splinters had penetrated the brain.

But they had started surgery in time, and when he had removed the last bits of bone from the brain and the coagulated blood had been sucked away, he knew that the girl would survive.

He stitched the skin with perfectly steady hands and saw the appreciative look in sister Elena's calm, kind eyes.

"That went well, doctor," she remarked as he rolled off the latex gloves and started to wash. "I hope we won't bother you more tonight." She sounded happy and encouraging. She had no idea of everything that lay behind him nor whatever lay before him.

"Thanks, sister. The patient should be monitored closely, and if something happens, I want to be notified immediately. But I don't expect any complications."

He smiled tiredly at her, then went to change clothes.

Back in his room, his hands started to shake again, and fatigue struck him with tremendous force. He sank into a chair and closed his eyes.

Life and death, life and death—an eternal chain. He had just saved a life, and he had just killed a man. He wondered who the man was...if there was a wife left behind, children...children who had lost their father?

He pulled out a drawer in his desk, got hold of a bottle, and poured himself a glass of whisky. His hands shook so bad that the amber drink spilled over his pants. But he didn't notice.

He emptied the glass in one gulp and went out into the corridor.

The two policemen waited on a couch. A nurse who was talking to them looked at him with anxious eyes.

"The police..." she started, but Pierre stopped her.

"I know." The glass of whisky had restored his confidence. He was prepared. "I will come."

The policeman with the sullen face looked at him for a moment before he said, "Come along now, doctor. We'd better take a BAC right away. You must have all the equipment here for a blood test, sister?"

Now Pierre understood. With the whiskey he spilled over his pants, the policeman must have felt the smell of booze.

"That's fine," he replied with a shrug. "Will you take the blood test, sister?"

The young nurse nodded. She looked scared, and he felt her fear rubbing off on him.

What were these men going to do with him?

He felt like an invisible net slowly closed around him as he followed the nurse to an examination room. The policemen kept close behind as if they feared that Pierre might try to run off.

But why would he try to escape? There was nothing to escape from.

Or...was there?

"I'm afraid," he said softly. "Terribly scared. Something will happen, and I will not get a second chance."

Pierre stared out the window. It had been three days since the accident with the man on the Interstate and three days filled with anxiety and despair. He had continued working at the hospital as if nothing had happened, his colleague Dr. Austen had returned from New York and eased the workload, but Peter Dahl was still at home with the flu. So this afternoon, he had come to visit Peter and Astrid Dahl in their beautiful house in Alexandria. They were his friends, and he wanted to consult them.

"You're just exaggerating," Peter said lightly and leaned back in the armchair. His narrow intelligent face smiled, but his eyes were serious. He had never seen Pierre so upset. "It was an accident. It could happen to anyone."

"The police did not seem to share your views. They thought I was speeding and could not understand that I didn't see the man in time to... They even took a blood test."

"And the result?"

"It's not final yet. But I think it will come out negative. I had been drinking a little, but that was earlier in the day. I had a late lunch with Clara and her father at Laurier's, we had a drink and a few glasses of wine, but I skipped the brandy with coffee. Later, at home, I had a glass of wine with Clara..." He sat silent for a moment, then pushed his fingers through the thick dark hair. "But later,

after the surgery at the hospital, I had a whisky. I was
tired and upset. I spilled whiskey on my pants, and the
smell must have made the cops suspicious."

"Who is analyzing the blood test?"

"Harrison. Emelie Harrison. She was very friendly
but seemed a little reserved. You know the expression: a
doctor on duty should not drink."

"But you weren't on duty. You had to come in
unexpectedly."

"I don't think that is taken into account."

Peter Dahl leaned forward.

"Do you want me to call Harrison? I have met with
her several times; maybe we can—"

Pierre shook his head. "No, Peter, I want this to be
legit. The law must have its course. And Clara…" He fell
silent and closed his eyes.

"What about Clara?" said Peter slowly.

"Well, she wanted to help me. She works for a big law
firm, and her father has significant influence. She claimed
we could easily get the entire case dismissed. And when
I disagreed, she wanted to engage Diana Benowitz as my
lawyer. But I can't afford Diana Benowitz, and I don't
want help from the Buschs."

Astrid Dahl had been quietly leafing through a
magazine, but now she suddenly exclaimed, "But that
man you hit—Julio Alvarado. The autopsy showed he
was drunk as a skunk that night. It must have been his
own fault.

"I went to find his widow the day after. They are
illegal immigrants from Nicaragua and live in a shack
on an abandoned… I wanted to offer her some financial

support, but she wouldn't listen to me. She was filled with hatred for the man who killed her husband and left her alone with three children, and besides that, she is prepared to swear that her husband was sober that night—as he always was."

"But, the autopsy results…" Astrid said.

"It's the kind of thing that a prosecutor like Josef Espina will make the jury disregard. You know he has a good eye for illegal immigrants but a not-so-good eye for doctors after his wife died three years ago. He is convinced that she could have been saved if it wasn't for medical malpractice. He doesn't realize they sought help too late."

"Do you know where Alvarado came from that night…or where was he going?" asked Peter Dahl, who began to understand that Pierre's situation wasn't quite as simple as he first had thought. If Josef Espina was the prosecutor, it wouldn't be easy for Pierre.

"The widow claimed he only went out to get some fresh air. She is prepared to testify to that," Pierre replied tiredly.

For a moment, Peter looked questioningly at his wife. Her eyes were as serious as his; she had also realized the dangers of the situation.

"When will the case be tried?" he said at last.

"In two weeks, I think."

"Have you got a lawyer?"

"No," Pierre shook his head. His face was pale and tired; it looked like he hadn't slept for a few nights. "I have hardly had time to gather my thoughts."

"Then I will contact Miranda Moore. She has done a lot for us at the hospital and is one of the best in D.C. She will help you. But we may also have to do some detecting ourselves. We must find out if anyone saw Julio Alvarado drunk that night. If we can find a witness, your position will immediately be stronger. I just don't know where to start."

Astrid Dahl closed the magazine and placed it on the coffee table. "How about the Alvarado widow? If you go together, you may be able to squeeze more information out of her."

The Alvarado widow was a plump woman of about forty. She received Pierre and Peter with cold silence, but her small black eyes began to sparkle when they presented their case.

"Is it not enough that you have killed my beloved Julio!" she exclaimed fiercely. "You also want to destroy his reputation. That will not do, doctor; my Julio was the kindest person in the whole world. He cared for us all, and if he ever had a drink, it was always just the one. Unlike others, who call themself doctors and run over innocent people in a drunken state."

Pierre's face turned white with anger, and Peter grabbed his arm.

"Come! Let's go," he said. "This is useless."

"Yes, go, you dirty pigs! And don't come back!" The agitated woman's shrill voice followed them as they passed the old yard where children played tag between rusty machinery.

”Killer!” The woman shouted from the doorway. ”You will get your punishment, doctor! I’m not giving in until you are behind bars. You dirty killers!”

The children laughed and shouted at them, and Pierre wondered which of them was Alvarado’s.

When they got back to Peter’s car, they heard a thin voice, and as they turned, they met a thin, frail man with a long gray beard and even longer hair.

”So, you are here again?” said the man Pierre recognized from his last visit. This man had pointed out which derelict shack the Alvarados lived in.

Pierre nodded, and Peter looked at the man with suspicion.

”She still claims that Julio was dead sober that night?”

”Yes,” Pierre muttered. ”And she is willing to testify.”

”She’s lying,” the old man grunted. ”Julio Alvarado was never sober. I think he was born with a bottle in his hand. But if you want to know more about what he did that night, you should visit the Ditch bar by the canal.”

”Is there a bar by the C & O Canal?” questioned Peter.

”There is an abandoned house at lock eleven,” explained the man. ”Not a regular bar but at night, there is a woman selling booze to the locals. Ask her.”

”Why are you telling us?” asked Peter Dahl, a little curious.

”I don’t like these freakin’ immigrants!” exclaimed the man loudly. ”They should pack up and go back instead of coming here taking honest American’s money.”

Pierre snorted and turned away. This man had probably never done an honest day’s work in his whole life and was just concerned with his own social welfare.

They went along the canal on Sunday night. The Chesapeake and Ohio Canal was an almost 200-year-old canal stretching over 180 miles from D.C. to Cumberland with over seventy locks. The locks were numbered starting at the capital, and number eleven was not far from the place of Pierre's accident.

The Lock house at lock eleven was abandoned and would soon be considered a ruin. The dark room was lit by battery-powered lanterns and an old cd-player squalled music. The smell of mold, urine, cheap booze, and marijuana made the two men stop momentarily before they entered.

A dozen men and a handful of women sat around small tables drinking from dirty glasses and smoking weed as well as tobacco. A black girl in her fifties, tall and voluptuous, stood behind a makeshift counter.

Pierre and Peter attracted many suspicious glances, but no one made a move to do something about these unusual guests; they were at least not cops.

"A man like Alvarado would fit right in here," Peter said. "This is his sort of crowd."

They approached the bar, and without a word, the woman placed two badly washed glasses on the counter and filled them with a colorless liquid.

"Why are you here?" she said suspiciously, resting her large black eyes on Pierre, but he didn't notice. His hand trembled when he reached for the glass. If he ever was to catch hepatitis, this was the place and time. He took a big gulp of the horrible and very strong liquor; it was foul.

"We are here to ask you about something," said Peter, leaning over the bar. "Did you know Julio Alvarado?"

The girl raised an eyebrow.

"Julio?" she said. "He who was killed on the Interstate some days ago?"

Peter nodded.

"Why do you ask?"

"Because it was my friend here who was in the accident," said Dr. Dahl bluntly. "And we want to find out where he came from that night … and if he was sober?"

"Sober?" The woman bent her head back and laughed, a deep dark laugh that filled the whole room. "Julio was never sober. And losing him was truly no loss to the world. Julio…sober…!" She laughed again.

"Do you remember if he was here that night?" asked Peter slowly.

She nodded.

"As soon as I opened the door, he was here. He owes me a lot of money."

"And he was drunk that night?"

"He was worse than usual. In the end, we had to throw him out. He was too rude, even for this crowd…imagine that, fellas."

"Would you be willing to testify to this in court?"

The girl suddenly looked frightened. "Why?"

"For my friend," Peter explained, nodding towards Pierre. "He is in a tight spot. They want to blame him for the whole accident."

The woman's eyes narrowed, and she looked at Pierre, who sat half-turned from the bar and stared emptily into the smoky room. Then she smiled.

"I will help you if I can. My name is Latonya. Latonya Williams. Call me when you need me, and I will come."

She turned and scribbled something on a piece of paper.

"This is my cell. I hope we can meet somewhere out of this horrible place…"

Now she looked intensely at Pierre.

When Pierre got home after dropping Peter off at the gate to the villa in Alexandria, he got the feeling that someone was in the apartment.

He hung up his jacket and stood momentarily, looking at himself in the entryway mirror. He looked tired. Peter had been full of enthusiasm over finding Latonya Williams and that she was willing to testify in Pierre's favor. Still, he could not share the friend's optimism. The feeling of an overhanging invisible danger did not leave him. It increased as he entered the living room and saw Clara sitting on the couch with her cell in hand.

She didn't smile at him.

She didn't fly up from her seat and wrap her arms around him as she used to, and her face was cold and upset.

"Well, there you are," she said. "Where have you been?"

He explained what he and Peter had accomplished in a few short words, but her expression did not change. The glare in the blue eyes became only even colder.

"What good do you think that bar girl will do when you are trialed by Thomas Kavanaugh?" she said mockingly. "You should have accepted my offer to be represented by Diana Benowitz. But only God knows if she would have a chance against Kavanaugh and Josef Espina.

"Thomas Kavanaugh?" Pierre exclaimed. "Judge Kavanaugh."

He closed his eyes, facing the unexpected blow. Judge Kavanaugh was famous and infamous in all of D.C. He was over eighty years old and should have retired long ago, but for some reason, he had managed to keep his post. He was a hard and intolerant old man with strong conservative beliefs, a judge known to rather convict than free, and notorious for his excessively severe judgments.

"Kavanaugh?" he repeated, walking over to the bar to pour them a drink. "But why? I thought he only got involved with criminal cases."

"Haven't you seen the latest news?"

He shook his head.

"I haven't been able to concentrate on anything lately, Clara." His voice was tense and tinged with despair, but the hard look on her face did not soften, and suddenly she looked like a complete stranger. Was this the girl he fell in love with? Was this the woman with the beautiful hard face he had dreamed a lot of foolish romantic dreams?

As he stood with their glasses in his hands watching her, he suddenly remembered that redhead outside Laurier's whose little boy he saved from being run over. He wondered if she was as cold and dismissing towards the man she loved? During these difficult days, her image had, for some inexplicable reason, popped up in his mind from time to time. He remembered her name: Lise Norrgard. Lise Norrgard, and her son Anders. They had been on their way to the airport to pick up her husband.

Clara had bent forward and held out her cell with the screen facing him. He noticed a page from a news site. Her voice was icy and impersonal when she started to read, and the words she read caused his fear to explode. He put down both glasses and stood motionless as he listened. His body felt icy cold, but the temples burned like a fever.

Drunk driving Washington D.C. doctor hit and killed an innocent pedestrian. Judge Thomas Kavanaugh accepted the case and stated, "A doctor under the influence of alcohol killed a fellow human being." This sensational trial will start next Wednesday. The prosecutor, Mr. Josef Espina, is said to have gathered strong evidence against the young doctor.

She dropped the cell phone and had tears in her eyes as she stared at him.

"Well, what do you say about that? And that is just the start. You should see social media! Twitter has a new trending hashtag, killerdoctor. It is time you pull yourself together, Pierre, and accept the help Dad and I offer you, before it's too late. Father could persuade the court to replace Kavanaugh, but it is too late to get the whole case dropped."

He looked at her in silence.

It would be so easy to take the hand she offered. That would free him from fear and anxiety.

But would he be able to carry on his life knowing that justice has not been allowed to take its course? Would he be able to look a single person in the eye if he let Mr. Busch help him escape a situation like this?

Again he thought of the beautiful woman with the green, peculiarly soothing eyes. Lise Norrgard. What would she think of a man who didn't face his responsibility?

He shook his head.

"Thanks, Clara, but I can't," he said. "I don't want to slip away. I know that I have not done anything criminal. It wasn't my fault that that man stumbled out on the road in front of my car. He had been drinking. We have evidence that he had been drinking. The girl—"

"That girl!" she exclaimed fiercely and stood up. "You're an idiot, Pierre! Someone like Judge Kavanaugh won't listen to a bitch who runs an illegal bar, and he will ensure that the jury does not attach any weight to her testimony. Besides, you don't know if she will show up."

"She said—"

Clara laughed, and it sounded evil. "Do you really believe in such promises?"

She stood still, looking at him. There was something final in her posture as if she said goodbye without expressing it in words.

"Once, I thought…" she said in a whisper. But she didn't finish the sentence. She turned around and left. He heard her put on her coat but did not follow her. The front door slammed shut.

Several minutes later, he found that she had left her key to his apartment on the small table in front of the sofa.

❤

Clara was right. When the trial began, the witness from the bar by the canal had gone missing. Miranda Moore, Pierre's lawyer, was confused—confused and depressed.

"She has disappeared into thin air," she said as they entered the courtroom. "Peter and I have done everything to try to get hold of her but to no avail. The bar is abandoned; just a few punks hang out there. One day she was there serving booze; the next, she was gone. And the cell number you got is no longer in use."

"But why?" Pierre stared at the lawyer.

Miranda shrugged.

"I don't know." She fell silent. She didn't want to say what she thought, but she was convinced that the prosecutor had a hand in the game—that it was Josef Espina who arranged that their main witness, the friendly Latonya Williams, could no longer speak in favor of Pierre Lyon-Cote. But there was one more thing that disturbed her piece. The autopsy reported that, clearly without unambiguity, Julio Alvarado had a large percentage of alcohol in the blood when he was run over—and it had gone missing. There was no copy. The police authorities apologized, but such things could happen. The bureaucracy was slow and overloaded: a lost report could be expected. Maybe it would turn up later.

She looked at Pierre and was filled with compassion, far from something she felt for every client. The young doctor seemed to have aged ten years over the past weeks. Miranda wanted to do everything in her power to help him, but she was not optimistic.

It wasn't just Judge Kavanaugh who gave her a sinister premonition. The composition of the jury also scared her.

She had tried to change it, but the only result was that two women were replaced by two other women. So the jury that would decide on "guilty" or "not guilty" now consisted of two-thirds of women—older women and housewives with husbands and children.

And it was unlikely that a jury of so many women would see her client's way after having made one of their fellow sisters a grieving widow with three small children.

The trial was a nightmare. It started at nine o'clock on Wednesday, and the small courtroom on the second floor of Moultrie Courthouse was packed to the breaking point. Many curious visitors had to be turned away.

Pierre tried to answer calmly and sober-mindedly to the questions addressed to him, but he felt a sense of unreality—as if he did not participate, as if he watched the whole thing as part of the spectators.

The Judge's withered old face remained expressionless during the initial negotiations. Miranda Moore fought hard to turn the jury's sympathies in favor of Pierre, but when the jurors, on the afternoon of the second day, retired for individual deliberations, everyone but Pierre knew that he was lost.

This was no ordinary traffic case. Somehow the prosecutor and the Judge had turned it all into a case of human responsibility, duty, and human rights.

Through insidious hints, the prosecutor made the accused appear in the darkest possible light, and the looks that Pierre received from the audience was no longer colored by curiosity and sympathy but by hostility and contempt.

It was as if he had given up the fight. He was no longer interested in the result. He was lost in dreams of his childhood in the small town far north of Quebec, about his parents who died when he was just a little boy, about the relatives who took care of him and helped him realize his calling to become a doctor and serve humanity.

He had worked hard and laboriously towards this goal. He had become a doctor. He had received scholarships. He had specialized in neurosurgery, studied for several years at American clinics, and where was he now?

A man who stood accused of being responsible for another man's death.

A doctor who failed his duty.

He hardly looked up when the jury returned and barely reacted when the chairman, a short, lanky man with a most ordinary appearance, read the jury's verdict.

There was a loud murmur in the audience when the word "guilty" was stated, but the buzz subsided after the Judge hit his mallet on the desk a few times.

"Doctor Pierre Lyon-Cote," the Judge said in a voice that felt like sandpaper, turning his stern gaze on Pierre. "I look very serious on the crime of which the jury found you guilty. Another Judge would perhaps look lighter on such crimes, and I have always aimed for justice during my many years in court. People must not forget their responsibilities. The day Julio Alvarado was killed, you had consumed a lot of alcohol. Despite that, you got into your car when called to the hospital. You have said that you called for a taxi, but you have not been able to prove this. You drove even though you must have known you were not in a fit state to drive a car."

"Doctor Lyon-Cote. You are a medical doctor, a tool in the service of humanity. You are a man who has dedicated your life to saving human life. Instead, you have taken a life. And I haven't been able to find any mitigating circumstances."

The Judge sat motionless and silent for a while, then turned to the jury.

"Dear jurors! You have arrived at the only possible decision. You have found the accused guilty of causing the death of another. Mrs. Alvarado"— he made a discreet bow towards the widow who sat sobbing in the front row—"is living proof of the hideous tragedy that occurred because of another man's lack of judgment. The court's decision is binding, and I hope it will set an example for those who think, feel, and act like Doctor Lyon-Cote. My ruling is as follows: The accused is found guilty of vehicular homicide under paragraph 50–2203.01 of the Code of the District of Columbia. I hereby sentence Dr. Pierre Lyon-Cote to one-year imprisonment and twenty-five thousand dollars in compensation to the widow."

A buzz went through the audience. Pierre stood immobile. The flicker before his eyes took the shape of whirling stars as the opening scene for Star Wars on acid. His hands clenched, nails dug into the palms, but he felt no pain.

The words were too terrible to be true.

Judge Kavanaugh cleared his throat and continued. "However, due to the nature of the crime, I want to reduce the sentence. The twelve months of imprisonment will be converted to six months suspended sentence so that the accused, in practice only, will serve six months in prison. If he, after completing the sentence, is found guilty of a similar offense. In that case, the six-month parole will immediately turn into unconditional imprisonment. I hereby declare the case between the District of Columbia and Doctor Pierre Lyon-Cote concluded. The sentence is decided, and the penalty shall be immediately enforced."

The nightmare was over, and the hell had just begun.

Pierre returned to his apartment while Miranda Moore pursued the case in a higher court.

The days flew by.

Peter and Astrid Dahl, Miranda Moore, and the hospital staff did everything to encourage him. The court's ruling was absurd. A higher instance would certainly overrule Kavanaugh's conviction.

But their words were of little comfort.

Pierre's fear only increased with each passing day. Spring came, the sun glittered in the Potomac River, and the birds sang joyfully in the blooming trees. When he stood on his balcony and saw their free flight from branch to branch, tree to tree, and beyond, he was paralyzed with anxiety.

The mere thought of being locked in a cell behind bars horrified him.

He repeatedly tried to go through what happened, but he could find no explanation. He had been sentenced to a year in prison. The Judge had been soft, and six months imprisonment had been converted to a suspended sentence on the condition that he promised penance and improvement and never again killed a fellow human being or committed a DUI offense.

So, what was his crime?

His nights were one constant torment of self-examination and self-condemnation. While he, during the days, threw himself into hard work to try to forget his brooding anguish. His hands were still steady with the surgical knife, but his thoughts were no longer working. In the middle of May, he resigned from the hospital under the pretext that he needed a period of leave.

On the twenty-seventh of May, he attended little Freyja Landry's funeral. He stood by the girl's grave and looked at the small white coffin, and his sense of impotence was greater than ever. She had been his patient, but he had not been able to help her.

She had died because he and his colleagues were incapable—because science could not save a small child with a barely visible tumor deep inside the cerebellum.

Freyja was dead.

Was he the killer, even in this case?

Two days later, he received the final blow.

"Pierre?" said the voice on the phone as he answered.

"Yes, it's me." The cellphone displayed Miranda Moore's name. "What do you want?"

"The ruling from the higher instance has come. Do you want me to come over and review it with you?"

His hand tightened its grip on the communication device. His eyes sought the blue sky, which opened in infinite freedom above his balcony window.

"You can tell me the phone, Miranda," he heard himself answer.

"Unfortunately, the ruling is negative," the lawyer stated after a moment's hesitation. "Do you think you are strong enough to hear this?"

"Continue."

"The Court of Appeal regrets the ruling. They see the sentence as unnecessarily strict, but, unfortunately, they have not found a reason to reverse it."

"And…what does that mean?" Pierre said softly.

"That the punishment remains. But don't worry. The battle is not lost yet. I have already initiated an appeal to the Department of Justice. The attorney general can, without further ado, get the sentence annulled, and he probably will too. He has an entirely different and significantly more liberal approach to our country's administration of justice than old Judge Kavanaugh. He will—"

Pierre was no longer listening. He had hung up.

The Department of Justice… Clara …

What was Clara doing just now?

They had not spoken again. Apparently, she had considered their breakup final. She had returned the key to his apartment. She no longer wanted anything to do with a man who refused her father's benevolence and help, a man whom the law had condemned as a cold-blooded criminal. A man who had been torn to shreds in the press and whose name was clued to a scandal.

Clara…

He slowly sang down on the large couch as his phone rang again, but he did not recognize the number. He heard a voice he had learned to hate and fear. The voice was formal but not unfriendly.

"Doctor Lyon-Cote," said the district attorney. "This is Josef Espina."

"I see," Pierre said with tension.

"You may have heard about the verdict by the Court of Appeal?"

"Yes, I was just informed."

"Good. Getting this done as soon as possible is probably just as well. That's why I'm calling."

"What… What do you want?"

"I have a proposal to make to you, Doctor Lyon-Cote. For your own good, you should accept. I'll give you until tomorrow. To avoid commotion and excitement from the media and public, I won't send the police to pick you up. If you come to my office tomorrow afternoon at four o'clock, I will arrange a discrete transport to the Correctional Treatment Facility so you can start serving your sentence immediately. Are you there, doctor Lyon-Cote?"

"Yes. Yes, I am here."

"And you have understood me? Tomorrow at four at my office."

"Yes," Pierre whispered. "I have understood."

That night he made his decision.

It was a decision that slowly had matured within him, but now it took clear form. He knew what he had to do.

He couldn't go to prison.

Miranda Moore had indeed promised to appeal to the Department of Justice, but the wheels of bureaucracy turned slowly. The decision could take a long time. And in the meantime, Pierre would slowly wither in a cramped cell with bars across the window.

As dawn came, he was washed, shaved, and ready. His suitcase was packed with the essentials, and he had looked up the train times, buses, and cheap car rentals.

He had time until four o'clock this afternoon. Only after four would the prosecutor raise the alarm, and the police would start looking for him.

He had carefully gone through everything.

A man who wanted to escape the U.S. law would most likely cross the border into Mexico. From Mexico, there were many escape routes to choose from. South America was big, and there were places deep in the jungle where countless people started new lives under new names. Down there, they didn't ask where a man came from or what he had done. He had purchased tickets to San Antonio, Texas online. That was close enough to the Mexican border and left a digital trace for the police to follow. But Pierre wasn't going to escape into the jungles of South America.

At a quarter past eight, he left his apartment, drove down to Laurier's, and parked in the parking lot for guests. It was like a repetition of something that had already happened. It was just that there was so much that had happened. A life had been changed—a life had been ruined.

The Amtrak to New York City was already on the track when he entered Union Station from the taxi. People streamed back and forth in the morning rush, and no one attached any importance to the tall, dark man who walked along the train and got on one of the front carriages. No one knew he was on the run from justice and that he burned all bridges.

Lake Sables—the lake of his childhood.

Neuveville—the town of his childhood.

It had been thirty years since he last visited, and now he was on his way back.

No one would think of looking for him there and he had made sure not to leave any traces—only cash purchases.

He looked at his seat ticket and searched for the compartment. The door was closed, but when he opened it and stepped in, he saw he was not alone.

A woman and a boy were sitting by the window. The boy didn't seem to have heard him, he was pressing his nose against the window, but the woman looked up, and her eyes widened.

For a brief second, they stood as if frozen, taking in the other's gaze, then she smiled and held out her hand.

"Hello, again," she said. "Do you remember me? I am Lise Norrgard."

Confused, he took her hand. It was calm and firm in his, a slender, powerful hand with confidence.

"Yes. Of course, I remember you, Mrs. Norrgard." He blushed slightly. "And I must have forgotten to introduce myself when we last met. You must have thought I was such a hick."

"Not at all," she said softly. "There was no reason. But maybe now, since it seems we are traveling together."

"Roy," Pierre heard himself say. "Eric Roy."

Eric Roy, he thought. Where did that name come from? Couldn't he have come up with something better?

It was a name that was so common among French Canadians that its mundaneness made it suspect, but when he looked at Lise Norrgard, she didn't seem to have any suspicions.

She sat and looked at him but did not smile, and her large green eyes looked sad. And then he noticed the subdued colors she was wearing. She had worn a green dress the last time they bumped into each other. Now she had a black turtleneck sweater and gray pants.

"You… Have you been through something sad since last we met, Mrs. Norrgard?" he asked awkwardly as he placed his luggage on the rack and sat across from her.

She nodded slowly, then looked at the boy with his nose pressed against the window exploring the seething activity on the platform.

"My husband," she said softly, then she put a finger to her lips and nodded towards the boy.

He understood. She didn't want to discuss what had happened, so the boy heard it. Her husband must have died, and the wound was still too fresh for her to talk casually about.

Pierre remembered that she, that time outside the restaurant, mentioned something about her son loving his father very much. And they were on their way to the airport to…

Suddenly it hit him. He hadn't forgotten Lise Norrgard, despite their brief first meeting. However, due to the concern and anxiety that marked his own time after the meeting, he had forgotten the news about the plane crash in Washington D.C.

Over ninety people perished in the disaster, one of the worst in recent history. Both crew and passengers were gone, and as his own situation had suddenly turned so serious, he had not been particularly interested. But he remembered that it had been something peculiar with the plane crash. The FAA accident investigation had not been able to come up with any plausible explanation. The weather had been good, the visibility over the region good, and the news had mentioned something about human error. But he did not know if the mystery surrounding the accident had been completely dispersed.

Had Lise's husband been on that plane?

Had Anders lost his father in that accident?

The train started moving with a soft jerk. Faces slipped past outside the window, they left Union Station and Washington D.C. behind them, and they were on their way north.

The boy turned and caught sight of him.

Pierre was shocked when he saw the child's face. He was much thinner than he remembered; the cheeks had lost all color, and the blue eyes looked huge under the blond curls.

"Do you remember me?" he said kindly and gave the boy a smile.

The boy stared at him gravely, then shook his head.

”I'm on my way to my grandmother's,” he said with a thin voice. ”She lives far up north…by a big lake. There are bears up there, and Dad promised me to see them. Bears! Like on TV. Dad will take me to them.”

He stopped suddenly and looked at his mother.

”Dad is coming, right?” he asked anxiously.

”We'll see,” Lise Norrgard answered softly. Her voice was warm and clear, but she couldn't completely hide the sad uncertain tone, and suddenly the boy's eyes were filled with tears.

”I want Daddy to come!” he exclaimed. “You can't fool me! We will greet the Indians that…”

He hid his face in his hands, and Mrs. Norrgard wrapped her arms around his small stiff body and pulled him close so the boy came to rest with his head in her lap.

”Try to sleep now, Anders,” she whispered. ”We have a very long journey before we get to Grandma. And you will certainly see the bears at Lake Sables.”

Lake Sables! Pierre flinched, feeling the uncertainty wash over him again. Why Lake Sables? Why not Ontario, Michigan…or Lake Winnipeg?

He had been so convinced that they would soon part ways, and now they were going to the same destination.

He calmed down a bit. Why would it matter? They knew nothing about him. They only knew that he traveled from D.C. and was called Eric Roy. They would not make the connection between him and a wanted doctor named Pierre Lyon-Cote.

He was Eric Roy. He was an engineer and had taken the summer months off to recover after severe pneumonia.

He noticed how quickly and easily his mind worked. One lie built another. He had never realized it was so easy to lie, but maybe it was easy for a man who deliberately burned every bridge after him and was on the run from the law.

Eric Roy.

He looked at the woman who tried to stroke her son to rest, and he suddenly wished he had never met Lise Norrgard.

The boy had fallen asleep and did not wake up when the conductor poked his head into the compartment and asked for the tickets.

Lise Norrgard saw, to her surprise, that Mr. Roy turned away his face as if he didn't want to be seen by the conductor. She registered a shadow of fear sliding over his thin sharp-cut face, but soon after, he was back to normal, and she told herself that she had just imagined things.

The train sped on through the sun-drenched landscape, and Lise rose, found a blanket, and placed it over the sleeping boy. She sat and looked at her son in silence for a moment, then she directed her green eyes at Pierre. They looked filled with grief and sadness.

"I didn't want to talk about my husband when Anders listened," she said softly. "He still hasn't realized that he will never get to see Michael again. Michael…was my husband."

Pierre nodded. "You don't have to talk about it, Mrs. Norrgard, if it bothers you."

"No, I would like you to know. That time when we met outside the restaurant in Washington D.C., Anders and I were on our way to meet my husband at the airport. He was working for the government and was on his way back after a long business trip to Europe, and we didn't often have the opportunity to meet because we still live up north. After the summer, we had plans to move to D.C.…."

She sat quietly for a moment, playing with the large golden ring that almost looked far too big for her slender finger, then she continued, barely audible. "We never got to meet my husband. The flight he was on crashed. We stood at the airport and saw how it crashed in a ball of fire. Anders got a severe shock, I had to take him to a doctor, and he was hospitalized for weeks. He loved his father very much." She swallowed hard. "I haven't been able to explain what happened."

"Sometimes it can be impossible to tell the truth," said Pierre thinking about his own situation. "Perhaps it is best to let time do the work and one day…"

"Yes, exactly," she said and looked at him, almost relieved. "I have tried to convince myself of that, but it's not easy. Michael and Anders…the relationship between them was very strong. Sometimes I felt I did not have a place in their relationship. My husband had a very vivid imagination—he built a world around them which he populated with fairy-tale characters. Sometimes I felt that it wasn't good for the boy to be so dependent on his father, but on the other hand, I could not deprive him of what Michael gave him. They met too rarely, and Anders literally worshiped him."

"One day, he will forget," said Pierre slowly, looking at the little five-year-old lying on his side with one hand under the cheek. His mouth was half open, and his long eyelashes rested over the pale, thin cheeks. "Children forget so quickly."

Lise Norrgard smiled, a sad, introspective smile, and he came to wonder how hard she took the man's death.

"And now you are going to Lake Sables?" he said after a little while.

She nodded.

"Michael's mother—my mother-in-law—she lives there," she said with a peculiar hard pull around the red lips. "She is disabled, and I thought I had to get up and help her through her grief. She has also taken it extremely hard. Michael was her only son."

He said nothing and looked at her.

She was very beautiful in a quiet, introspective way and probably also very strong.

It was as if he saw her with new eyes. He liked what he saw but wished he had met her under other circumstances.

For her, he would always be Eric Roy—unless something unexpected happened.

He would rather have met her as Pierre Lyon-Cote.

They arrived at Neuveville late at night. The journey lasted more than twenty hours. They had changed trains in New York City, and the last three hours were spent on a bus. Endless forests with huge larches and firs had replaced the fertile fields in the south, and they had seen white spots glimmering here and there among the trees—snow that the spring sun had not yet melted.

Lise Norrgard turned up her jacket collar as Pierre carried the little boy down from the bus and helped them to a taxi.

No one was there to meet them, but Lise had explained that her mother-in-law was disabled.

"You don't have someone to meet you?" she asked when he placed the boy into the taxi, and she turned around to say goodbye.

She looked up into Pierre's face. She was tall, but he was a few inches taller, and when she saw his friendly gaze, she felt sad to part with him.

He had listened to her during the long hours on the train and hadn't troubled her with unnecessary questions. Somehow it was as if he understood her, and it was as if he had a place in her life, although they had only known each other for less than a day. And now they were to part.

"No, I have no one to meet me," he replied, and she noticed how he quickly turned to look at something across the street. A policeman had entered the bus station. He was dressed in the red uniform of the mounted police, and the beige wide-brimmed hat stood out in the small crowd around the bus. She wondered if Mr. Roy was afraid of the policeman or just saw something interesting that she could not notice. But Eric Roy's eyes soon met hers again, and he looked tired.

"I was only five years old when I moved away," he said, glancing over the yellow station house, "and I hardly remember anything about the town. And there is no one here who remembers me. My parents died, and I had to move to relatives in southern Canada."

"Have you decided where you will stay?" Lise asked as she held out her hand.

He shook his head. "I guess I have to rent a room somewhere," he said indifferently. "It shouldn't be difficult. The winter season is ending, and the summer's tourist invasion has hardly set in yet."

She looked up at him. There was something that worried him, but she didn't understand what. She didn't want him to feel uneasy. She wanted him to smile and be happy. He had hardly smiled once during the trip, and his eyes had a hunted expression.

"Will we meet again?" she asked softly.

"Probably," he replied. "The town's not big. We can hardly avoid bumping into each other."

He stood silent for a moment, then continued softly, "Maybe I could arrange for Anders to see the bears. If I remember correctly, there is a place on the other side of the Lake."

"Oh, Mr. Roy, that would be delightful." She paused for a while, then asked for his cell phone. "Let me give you my number, and you can call me if you want?"

He nodded.

But when she got into the car and he saw the taxi drive away, he knew he didn't want to see her again.

She was too much of a risk.

It was past midnight.

Eight hours ago, the hunt for Pierre Lyon-Cote had begun. He took his suitcase and left the bus station. The policeman in the red uniform was not to be seen. Maybe he was waiting somewhere in the dark.

Pierre had been shocked when the policeman appeared at the station. Why was he there? It looked as if he studied the few passengers that had just arrived, but it could be a matter of routine. There were still shady people who wanted to seek shelter in the wilds of Canada—people who, like himself, were on the run—people who still believed the stories of gold and precious stones in the vast wastelands.

But if the policeman was on the lookout for a fugitive doctor from Washington D.C., he would not have found him. The runaway doctor would travel alone, but the passengers who disembarked at Neuveville had all been in couples or families. Pierre was suddenly grateful to Lise Norrgard and her son. They had unknowingly given him a sort of camouflage when he needed it most. The policeman had not been interested in a group of three—a man, a woman, and a small child.

But the fear lay like a wet blanket over him as he walked up the narrow street toward the central part of town.

The houses lined the street looked like pictures from a photo album for him. He remembered some of them but not all. Some were old and had probably been around during his time, two-story brick houses mixed with the odd wooden house, which probably originated from the time of the gold rush at the end of the last century. Had he lived with his parents in a home like that? He didn't know.

Neuveville was his childhood town, but his childhood had ended so abruptly. He had been the same age as little Anders when he lost his father and his mother and his childhood with them.

His thoughts were spinning as he walked. He wondered what Clara was doing. Did she feel hate and contempt for him because he did not stay in D.C., and faced his responsibility? Could anyone understand why he acted as he did? Could Peter and Astrid Dahl, his best friends, sympathize with the panic that gripped him when he heard about the prosecutor's transport to the prison? Could they forgive him?

He came up to Rue du Pont, the town's main street. Apart from a few men having a smoke outside a tavern, the street was empty. They did not notice him as he passed. There seemed to be an argument as they sounded upset. He hurried on as he did not want to be present if there was a fight and the police were called.

He came up to a yellow two-story house surrounded by a large garden. In the light above a small sign, insects swarmed; the sign said ROOMS FOR RENT.

The light was on in a ground-floor window, somewhere a dog barked in the night as he opened the gate and walked up the gravel path. Stones crunching under the soles of his feet.

There was still snow under the bushes, but some sleepy flowers had greeted the spring in the flower bed close to the house. Soon the days would be longer, and spring would quickly pass by and be replaced by Canada's blooming short summer. When he knocked on the door, he felt strangely as if he had come home, and he just wished that the people who advertised ROOMS FOR RENT would let him stay.

His fatigue suddenly felt unlimited.

The room was on the upper floor. It was large, bright, pleasantly furnished, and had a view of Lake Sables with the blue mountains in the distance.

The hosts did not ask any questions. Mrs. Cameron, an elderly shapeless woman with swollen legs and a friendly face, welcomed him as an old friend. Her husband, a retired truck driver, offered to follow on fishing trips on the lake as often as he wanted.

He paid the rent a month in advance and agreed with Mrs. Cameron that he should have breakfast in the room and other meals he would eat in the town.

It was almost morning when he slid in under the duvet. Despite the fatigue, he could not fall asleep. He stared up into the darkness, and suddenly, his body started to tremble as if in convulsions. He thought he heard Judge Kavanaugh's dry, bored bureaucratic voice say, "I hereby sentence Dr. Pierre Lyon-Cote to one-year imprisonment and twenty-five thousand dollars in compensation."

He pressed his hands to his ears to block out the terrible words, but it was in vain. He heard them over and over again. They hammered against his temples, they tore at his nerves, and he whispered to himself, "Pull yourself together. You cannot fall apart. You have left all that behind you, and no one knows where you are. No one will guess that you took a retreat in this remote part of the country. No one will look for you here."

Sweat broke on his forehead, and when he realized he would not fall asleep, he got up and stood by the window, looking out on the small town.

The thoughts were suddenly on the beautiful redheaded woman with sad green eyes.

Lise Norrgard would never break down. She would not have allowed malicious, intolerant people without hearts to crush her. She was strong. She must have loved her husband but had not been put down despite him being brutally and unexpectedly torn from her. She held herself together for the sake of her son. She had even made this long journey to be with her husband's mother and relieve her of grief and pain.

The thought of Lise Norrgard calmed him. He was determined to stay out of her way, not to meet her again, but he didn't have to stop thinking of her.

He went back to bed.

"I'm Eric Roy," he whispered into the darkness where he lay between clean white sheets that smelled faintly of lavender. "I am a man with no past and an undetermined future. There are people with greater sorrows than mine. If they can manage, so can I…"

A moment later, he was sleeping peacefully.

He had come home—even if this home was no more than a temporary refuge.

For three days, nothing happened. He started browsing the news every morning as he enjoyed Mrs. Cameron's breakfast. He found nothing. No reports, no alerts, no warrants. Not even in the D.C. news. The news was full of reports from around the world. There were murders and accidents, bank robberies and embezzlements, but nothing about a fugitive doctor from Washington D.C.

He didn't understand it.

Why hadn't they announced a warrant for him right away? After all, he was found guilty of causing another man's death; he had been convicted. He had fled before they had time to lock him up in a cell. In the eyes of the law, he was a dangerous criminal who must be captured at all costs and sent to his punishment. So, why was nothing written about him?

Had they still not noticed his escape? They must have realized that as soon as he failed to appear at the prosecutor's office.

Maybe the newspapers considered the case so insignificant that it wasn't worth reporting?

On the fourth day, he saw it and almost felt relief. It read:

Fugitive doctor wanted by the police.

Doctor Pierre Lyon-Cote, a brain surgeon from Saint Orbona Hospital in Washington D.C. sentenced to DUI after hitting and killing a pedestrian on the Interstate in the capital, has suddenly disappeared before starting to serve his sentence. The US police suspect that he crossed the border into Mexico. Doctor Lyon-Cote is thirty-five, six foot two tall, and has dark hair. Anyone who

He let the cell phone drop. He was sitting on the edge
of his bed with coffee and a sandwich that he had not
tasted yet, and now his appetite was gone. He got up,
dressed, and left the house. It was almost noon, and the
streets of the small town were filled with people going
about their business.

Pierre walked among them with a feeling of being
watched from all sides. There must be more than he who
had read that small news item—would they recognize
him?

He entered the general store and found a pair of
shades, horn-rimmed with dark smoke-colored lenses.
He decided to stop shaving and grow a beard; not shaving
this morning was a good start.

He went down to the lake and walked for hours
along the narrow dirt roads and paths. All snow was
gone on the sunny beaches, and the sand was white and
fine and stretched into the sparkling dark blue waters.
Behind the beach, the forest grew dense, giant green firs
and deciduous trees swelled with buds. In a few days,
everything would be intensely green, and when the sun
rose higher, it would warm the water, and people would
come to the lake to swim.

He met no one, and he was grateful to be alone.

The news item had brought relief, but it had also
brought a threat. He knew now that they were searching
for him, though it seemed they were searching in the
wrong place.

The article had been vague. It had been objective, reporting and did not come with any condemnations, yet it had been missing one significant part. He had not been drunk when he hit Julio Alvarado. It was Alvarado who had been drunk. Alvarado had stumbled into the highway and got killed; he had probably never known what hit him.

But no one could prove this. Bar, the woman who promised to testify to Pierre's favor, had disappeared, and he wondered where she was. Maybe she was back in the city now as she was no longer a threat to prosecution?

He stopped under a tree, sat down, and looked over the water for a long time, letting the thoughts rest.

The trial had been a farce, a joke on justice and the individual's legal certainty, but they had not been able to prove it. Pierre was charged and would remain a convict unless the Attorney General found good grounds to change the sentence—and that prospect was distant.

Pierre returned to town.

He went up to his room. His hosts were in the kitchen, and he shouted a greeting to them as he went up the stairs.

His heart pounded as he closed the door behind him. He was home and safe in his room. No heavy hand had been laid on his shoulder to drag him back to justice in the USA.

He went to the window to let in some fresh air, but at the last second, he stopped himself.

Fear washed over him as a hot wave when he saw the man who entered through the gate.

It was the policeman he had seen at the bus station. Still dressed in the red jacket, black breeches, and beige hat.

He stopped for a moment inside the gate and looked up at the house. Pierre quickly withdrew behind the curtains.

He saw the policeman walking up to the house, and soon after, he heard a knock on the door.

He stood motionless for a brief second, then quickly walked to the door and opened it ajar. He needed to know what the policeman wanted.

Had he come for him?

Had they located him after all?

"I'll get it!" he heard Mr. Cameron call to his wife.

And then he heard the old man's hurried steps coming into the entry hall, just below where he stood listening.

Pierre stood motionless, listening. His nerves were on edge, tense, and the anxiety was almost nauseating.

The policeman in the red uniform must be after him; there was no other explanation. He must have found out that there stayed a mysterious guest at Cameron's B&B—a man named Eric Roy who was, in fact, wanted by the police in Washington D.C. for vehicular homicide.

He heard Mr. Cameron fumbling with the lock, and Pierre grabbed the doorpost for support.

"Hello, Jonathan," he heard the old man say downstairs. "What have we done to be honored of a visit by the mounties? They haven't reported me for illegal fishing, have they?"

Pierre could hear the policeman try something of a laugh, but it sounded more like an angry growl.

"Not yet, Barnard. This regards a completely different matter. Can I come in?"

"Sure, sure." The old man stepped aside to swing the door open. The draft sent a chilly breeze up the stairs to the upper floor, and Pierre noticed his forehead was wet with sweat. His hand closed tightly on the doorpost when he heard the policeman enter the house.

"Let's go into the living room," said Mr. Cameron. "The kitchen is a mess. Mollie is baking cornbread. Can I offer you a glass of something?"

Pierre leaned forward and saw the two men pass into the living room. The door closed behind them, and he couldn't hear the discussion that followed. He was alone with his fear.

He went into his room and closed the door quietly. His eyes searched the room for an escape route. Should he gather his things, pack, and sneak out of the house while the two men talked in the living room? Could he make it?

Probably not.

If the policeman had come for him, he would be on his guard as soon as he heard that the guest was in. The old wooden staircase to the ground floor creaked, and the policeman would listen for any sound.

He returned to the window and pressed his forehead against the glass, but the soothing cold on his skin did not release his nervous tension. It felt as if every muscle was tied in a cramp.

Only now did he realize what it meant to be on the run. A prey for hunters.

He sank down on a chair. His hands shook, and he folded his hands to keep them still. The agonizing wait was excruciating, and the hands of his watch hardly moved. But when he heard a door on the ground floor opening, more than ten minutes had passed.

He ran to his door and listened.

The two men laughed.

He could hear the policeman's rough voice and Cameron's weaker voice, but he could not hear the words.

They laughed.

Was that a good sign or just a sign of the policeman's success?

He did not dare to open the door for fear that they would hear him, but a few seconds later, the front door slammed shut, and he could hear footsteps on the gravel path.

The policeman left the house.

Pierre ran quietly to the window to confirm. It was true. The red coat was already on the street and strolled leisurely up Rue du Pont.

What had Cameron told him? How did he persuade him to leave Pierre alone?

He sat down on the bed. His mouth was as dry as a desert, and he felt sick. The whole room seemed to sway, and he lay down and buried his face in the pillow.

He must calm down. He needed to pull together. Then he could go down and investigate what the policeman wanted.

The Camerons were sitting at the kitchen table when he came downstairs. A large pile of golden yellow crispy cornbread stood between them, and Mrs. Cameron was just serving tea from a white and blue teapot.

"Mr. Roy!" she exclaimed, smiling. "Maybe you want to taste? I just finished the cornbread, and it is more than enough for all of us."

He shook his head. Cornbread had been a favorite since childhood, but he had no appetite. He tried to make his voice steady:

"No, thank you, Mrs. Cameron. It is very kind, but I'm on my way out. Could you help me sew this button in my jacket, but I might come at a bad time…in the middle of tea?"

"Not at all. It is quickly done." The old woman stood up and took his jacket and the button he ripped off moments ago. She retrieved her sewing basket from a cupboard.

"Have a seat," Cameron said cheerfully and pulled out a chair for him.

Pierre sat down. He thought they should be able to see how nervous he was, but no one reacted.

Mr. Cameron enjoyed a large bite of the bread he dunked in the tea while Mrs. Cameron sewed the button.

Pierre sat quietly. He didn't know how to begin. If he got straight to the point, it could make them suspicious.

The woman came to his rescue.

"Bernard is so pleased," she said, leaning over the jacket. "Imagine that they have asked him to play. And he hasn't played in public for years."

"Play?" Pierre said, baffled.

"Yes, Bernard plays the trumpet. He used to play in a brass band when we were young, but he had to quit when the truck driving kept him away for weeks."

She gave her husband a loving look.

"It must have been the Police Superintendent who remembered," she said to her husband.

"The Superintendent?" Pierre looked at her.

"Yes, Constable White, Jonathan White came by and asked if Barnard wanted to play with them on Saturday. One of the regulars has fallen ill, and the police band has a concert at Vieux-Port on Saturday afternoon. And now they have asked Bernard, but I am not sure he should have accepted."

"Nonsense! One time cannot be dangerous."

"But you also have to rehearse with them."

"I have lungs like a horse," said Mr. Cameron and grinned at Pierre. "You get that from being outdoors fishing on Lake Sables."

"But that doesn't cure chronic bronchitis," muttered the old lady.

Pierre returned his smile, but he couldn't comment. The relief had been so unexpected, and he felt weak in his legs. But he managed to get up and thanked Mrs. Cameron for the jacket she handed him.

She followed him to the door.

"I have thought of something, Mr. Roy. If you want, I will be happy to take care of your laundry. A few items more or less do not matter."

"Thanks, thank you, that was kind," Pierre muttered. "But it is not necessary. I hand in the laundry to Laverie Chang," he lied.

"Well, then," said Mrs. Cameron, shrugging her shoulders. "If you change your mind, I would love to."

"Thanks, it will not be necessary."

He almost ran from the house.

He took a sigh of relief. He had had enough presence to decline her offer. At the last second, he remembered the small monograms that Clara had marked his shirts with in a fit of domesticity.

Mrs. Cameron would probably have been confused when she noted that Eric Roy's shirts were marked with the initials *PLC.*

As he walked to the town center, he decided to remove all monograms the same evening.

It was safer that way.

And one more link to the past would be broken – maybe even the final link.

❤

Fourteen days later, summer arrived. It was as if the sun had opened up and grown, flooding its life-giving warmth over the woods, mountains, and lakes.

Spring in these northern parts of Canada was vague and hesitant, but summer came in a blast. It seemed as if nature was in a hurry to live, as if time was so short before the winter shadows would settle over the country again.

Lise Norrgard sat with her mother-in-law on the porch outside the house. She swung the rocking chair slowly and listened to Beth's knitting needles clattering. The old woman was knitting a cardigan for Anders—the third in the short time they'd been here.

Anders was playing in a pile of sand inside the gate. On the other side, a steady stream of people passed by, young girls in light dresses, rough workers who came down from the forests, and some of the First Nations.

Anders was still silent and closed up, marked by the shock of his father's death. Perhaps he still didn't comprehend what happened during those terrible moments at the airport, but he had stopped asking when his father was coming.

"You still haven't heard anything about insurance?" Beth asked without stopping the knitting.

Lise shook her head. "You know that," she replied. "You bring in the mail every day."

"You received two letters yesterday." As usual, the mother-in-law's voice sounded slightly irritated when she addressed Lise. Beth could not use her legs, the Personal support worker Ana, a tiny Philippine woman in her fifties, had to carry her to and from the wheelchair. But she had compensated for her deficiency in other ways, her eyes seemed to notice everything happening around her, her tongue was sharp and mean, and she spared no one in her surroundings. And she seemed to have a sixth sense that read other people's thoughts.

Lise did not like her, and she scared her. But she had decided to stay the summer and intended to follow through, although the difficulties had begun to loom around her.

When she came here, she imagined Beth needed someone to support her during her grief, but she was wrong. Beth had taken her son's death surprisingly well though Lise had a nasty feeling that she somehow blamed Lise for it. Had she perhaps instinctively learned the truth about Lise and Michael? Had Michael hinted something to his mother?

"You know very well who those letters were from," she answered calmly.

"How can I know that? You tell me nothing. Just took them to your room and read."

Lise slowly rocked in her chair and made an effort to keep her voice calm and low.

"One letter was from my sister in Copenhagen. She invited us to come, she can give me a good job. The second was from an old schoolmate. I told you that at lunch."

"Copenhagen? What are you going to do in Copenhagen? It is a city of sin in a perverted country. When the insurance comes, you can stay here. I have the right to have my only grandchild close, for the short time I still have." Her voice whined with self-pity.

"First, we don't know if there will be any insurance money," replied Lise. "The investigation is not finished, and the papers for Michael's life insurance had not been filed in time, so there might not be any money at all."

"Nonsense!" snorted Beth. "Michael was a respected member of the public office, and of course, the insurance money will be paid."

Of course, Lise thought bitterly, *your son is so perfect, yet he was guilty of more than one wrongdoing. He cheated on me with different women around the world, and he drank. The office warned him several times about his behavior, but you don't know that. To you, he was perfection but to me …*

She did not follow through on the thought but hastily rose from the rocking chair, ran down the garden path, and opened the gate, but when she came out into the street, the tall, dark man was gone.

He had walked quickly, almost as if on the run. For a moment, he had looked up at the house, and she was convinced that he must have seen her, recognized her. So why had he rushed away so hastily?

She remained outside the gate and felt a dull sorrow. Why hadn't he stopped and waited until she could talk to him? Why hadn't he called? Was the connection she had felt between them only a delusion on her part? And he had almost promised to take Anders to see the bears on the other side of the lake.

She went back into the garden. She could see her mother-in-law's searching gaze from the porch, so she stopped by the sand heap and took Anders's dirty hand.

"Come on," she said. "It's getting late. I will fix you a glass of warm milk, and then it's time for bed."

The boy nodded in silence.

He obediently followed his mother, his little hand securely anchored in Lise's, but Beth didn't let her escape.

"Why did you run into the street?" she asked sharply.

Lise couldn't help blushing. "I thought I recognized someone," she replied. "But I was mistaken."

"Recognized someone? Who? I thought you did not know anyone in Neuveville?"

"It was the man from the train," the child said with a clear voice. "I recognized him too. But he didn't see me."

"The man from the train?" repeated Beth slowly. Her sharp piercing eyes didn't let go of Lise.

"Mr. Roy," said Lise. "Eric Roy. We met him on the train coming here. Once he stopped Anders from running into the traffic. That was in Washington D.C."

"Why haven't you told me?" Now her gaze was filled with undisguised curiosity.

"Maybe I didn't think it was worth mentioning," Lise replied calmly. She had regained her composure.

The sight of Eric Roy hurrying past without saying hello had shaken her, but now she had regained control.

"It was all so brief," she added, leading Anders inside.

A warm, friendly wind came from the southwest and made the crown of the great maple tree move in a dancing rhythm across the blue sky.

Pierre lay on his back and looked up at the tree with eyes wide open. The water in the lake was still cold and had bit his skin when he took a long swim. Now he lay in the sun-warmed sand and felt the blood pump through the body.

This was his favorite place. It was several miles from town and the resorts where quite a few summer guests had already checked in. He was at peace here. No one bothered him with unwanted questions. No one filled him with fear after curious snooping. The only sound that was heard was the soothing of the wind in the treetops and, now and then, the hard rapid wing beats of a duck or goose who flew close over the water's surface.

His thoughts wandered slowly and lazily in different directions. He wondered with a touch of sadness, what Clara did right now? Was she still with the Justice Department? It would not be unexpected if she left after the scandal with her ex. All her colleagues and friends knew she had been engaged to the doctor who had fled his prison sentence.

He also wondered how the widow Alvarado and her three children were doing. He had sent her a large check a few days before his escape, but he didn't know if she had cashed it. Maybe she was too proud to accept money from the man who caused her husband's death.

He closed his eyes, and the image of Lise Norrgard, as she sat on the porch outside that house, came to him with painful clarity. The woman in the wheelchair next to her must have been her mother-in-law.

He had seen Lise get up and run towards the gate when she recognized him but did not have the courage to face her. It had been several weeks since he read the news item about himself; after that, all had been quiet. The media had lost interest in his case, but he knew the police were still looking, and he didn't want to drag Lise into something that could become painful and difficult for her. It was best they didn't meet again.

But it had hurt to run away from her, and now he wondered what she had been thinking. Had she realized he had seen her but not wanted to meet her?

"Hello," someone said close to him.

He winced and opened his eyes. It scared him whenever he was addressed, and he sat up quickly.

Little Anders stood beside him, wearing blue swimming trunks, and his small, slender body was pale.

He quickly looked around. The boy's presence must mean that Lise was not far away.

"Hi," he replied, smiling uncertainly. "Where is your mom?"

The boy pointed toward a large boulder that almost divided the beach.

"She's sitting over there. We didn't know that you were here. We arrived a while ago."

He started bouncing the red ball he held.

"Do you want to kick the ball? Mom was tired, and it's no fun being alone."

Pierre hesitated momentarily, then stood up and brushed off the sand. He was already quite tanned.

"Come then!" he said, holding out his hands.

Anders laughed, then awkwardly threw the ball at Pierre. Pierre caught it and kicked it back, but the boy missed, and the ball rolled down to the water.

The sand was warm and soft under their feet. Pierre continued to play with the boy while he was constantly aware that Lise would see him at any time. How would she react? Was she disappointed with him? Would she call Anders and set off home when she discovered who the boy played with?

"What have you done since we got here?" he asked the boy when they took a break from kicking.

"Eh, nothing special," replied the boy. "Grandma is so strict. But Ana bakes good buns. But there is no one to play with, and I'm not allowed to go outside the gate. Not alone. Grandma says the traffic is dangerous. She doesn't understand that no one is driving cars on the sidewalk," he added matter-of-factly.

"She is probably just afraid that you will forget and run out into the street," said Pierre lightly. "Like that time in Washington D.C…"

"I don't do that anymore!" Anders exclaimed. "That time, I was in a hurry to meet…" He broke off abruptly, turned away, and started bouncing the ball hard on the sand.

He obviously knows, thought Pierre. He has understood that he will never see his dad again. And he was filled with a surprising tenderness for the boy who had been so attached to a father he would never see again.

"Mr. Roy!"

He turned around. Lise Norrgard stood a few yards away. She wore a white beach dress highlighting the slender body's soft curves, and her face had turned red. Was it from the sun, or by the surprise of meeting him here?

Pierre bowed slightly.

"We were playing," he said. "Anders found me, and we played soccer."

He suddenly found it hard to find the right words.

She came up to him, her green eyes were calm and clear and held no reproach.

"If he bothers you…" she began.

"No, no, he doesn't bother me at all," Pierre hurried to answer. "We had fun, didn't we?" He looked at Anders for support.

She smiled quickly.

"I thought you avoided our company, Mr. Roy."

He blushed and looked down. He felt strangely stripped to his swimming trunks, almost naked, but it was not the body that he was ashamed to show her. He got the feeling she was looking straight into him. But she didn't look angry, rather a little amused and wondering.

"I owe you an apology, Mrs. Norrgard. I—"

"You don't have to apologize. And please call me Lise. I'm from Denmark, and we are not as formal as you are."

He smiled. But once again, he felt he was being pushed into something he would prefer to avoid.

Some kind of trap.

"Anders seems to have recovered quite well," he said with a low voice a moment later. They sat on her blanket behind the boulder that provided protection from the wind.

The boy played by the water's edge, and Lise's eyes followed his movements.

"He is a peculiar child," she said. "I do not understand everything that goes on in his little brain. I think he has realized that his father is dead but does not quite understand what dead means. A five-year-old with his whole life ahead of him can hardly believe a person is gone forever. But he never mentions his father. The other day he burst into tears when his grandmother mentioned Michael in his presence, and I had a very hard time calming him down again."

Pierre nodded.

"And your mother-in-law? How is she?"

To his surprise, he saw Lise's face turn rigid in a grimace she could not hold back. She shrugged.

"She loved her son. Maybe she thinks I do not grieve for him enough." Her voice was expressionless, and she ran her hand over her white dress. "She got angry when I stopped wearing the black clothes, but it's summer, and I can't wear them in this heat."

He understood that she did not see eye-to-eye with her mother-in-law and that it was not easy for her. Suddenly he heard himself say, "I promised to show Anders the bears. Maybe we can arrange that?"

She looked gratefully at him.

"Do you think? Oh, that would be wonderful! Anders would be delighted."

"My host has a boat. He could get us across Lake Sable, but that's an excursion over several days, requiring a lot of preparations. We must have equipment, weapons…there are not only bears up there, and we have to be prepared."

Her eyes sparkled, looking like she was filled with new life.

"And how will we sleep?"

"Mr. Cameron—my host—told me there are good camping spots. People hike up there and go hunting, and there are rangers that can guide us."

"Do you think there are Indians there too?"

"Maybe, once there was a great Algonquin tribe in this area." He smiled and stroked a finger over his nose. "My family claims we have Algonquin blood in our veins. My great-great-grandfather came from France in the nineteenth century. He was a bachelor and married an Indian girl. It is said in my family that she was a princess." He smiled. "In any case, she had a lovely name, Weetamoo."

"Weetamoo?" Lise repeated slowly. He was amazed at how soft and melodious the strange name sounded over her lips.

"Yes, it means 'she who speaks to them,' and I guess it is why she could talk to my ancestor."

They looked at each other, and he thought her eyes had more shine than ever before.

"Can I tell Anders about this?" she asked.

"Of course." He nodded. "I'll talk to Mr. Cameron this evening."

They got up. She stood for a moment, looking up at him. The tan suited him. He looked less tired and worn out than when she met him on the train. In time the tan would become darker and more intense. Then he would resemble his ancestors even more with that big nose. But no Indians grew such a thick black beard in a few weeks; it too suited him, and she liked that he kept it trimmed.

"You…you have made me very happy, Eric," she whispered close to him. "And I don't know how to thank you."

Her eyes teared up, and she quickly turned away and called out to her son.

Pierre's worry was gone. He just felt happy that he suggested the trip, happy that she accepted it with such delight.

He had introduced himself to her under a false name, but that may not matter. He could give her and her son a few days of peace and escape from everyday life. After, he could retreat and leave them.

He felt surprisingly light at heart.

He had no idea that the acquaintance with Lise Norrgard and Anders would prove fatal.

They walked along the beach toward town, and Pierre felt calm and happy for the first time in a long time.

Anders held him by the hand, stopping now and then, and eagerly looked up at him as he asked some questions. Pierre had no idea that a five-year-old could be so curious. Still, he tried to answer the boy's questions as correctly and exhaustively as possible. At the same time, he tried to express himself so that the boy would understand.

Lise smiled when she found them falling behind, and she had to stop and wait for them.

"He doesn't tire you, does he?" she smiled at Pierre.

"Not at all." Pierre squeezed Anders's hand. "But he says he's hungry. I wonder…" He looked questioningly at her. He did not understand himself. He should beware of these people. They could be dangerous to him, and in the same way, he could become dangerous for them. And he didn't want to hurt them. But yet he continued. "I wonder if I couldn't invite you to a late lunch? Hotel L'Escale at the Promenade serves lovely fish, and Anders could have a burger. He told me that he loves burgers."

Lise was silent for a moment. She wondered what her mother-in-law would say. Beth would become mad if they didn't come home for dinner, but she was suddenly filled with defiance and an almost unleashed desire to spend more time with this serious man who had won Anders's confidence. For once, she wanted to ignore her mother-in-law.

"I… I don't really know," she said slowly. "It is very kind, but…"

"Oh, Mom! Please! I haven't had a burger since we got here. Grandma says it is too expensive!" Anders ran up to her, threw his arms around her, and looked up at her with big blue eyes.

She smiled and stroked his hair.

"All right, then. But you must promise to behave so you don't embarrass Uncle Eric."

The boy nodded eagerly, and a moment later, they arrived at the Promenade. It was a wide paved avenue lined with tall trees. Under the trees were white benches where summer guests enjoyed the warm sun. Large red flowers shone like fireballs in concrete flower pots. Fountains splashed water in the small, well-kept park surrounded by roses.

People were eating in the hotel garden, and Lise stopped to read the menu on a display stand at the entrance.

Pierre looked at the guests at the tables, and suddenly he froze and turned away.

Three women sat at a table close to the music pavilion, and he instantly recognized one of them.

Sister Elena! Elena Rudenko, his own surgical nurse. What was she doing here? He tried to remember, as the past hit him with incredible force. It felt as if he had been punched in the pit of his stomach.

Did sister Elena use to take her holidays at this time? And why had she never told him she used to visit Neuveville on Lake Sable?

He wondered if she had seen him. Probably not. Sister Elena was very impulsive; she would have waved and run to him immediately. They had always been good friends at work. She was his best surgical nurse and had faithfully stood by him throughout the trial. When the verdict came, she was very upset. Elena was one of the few who realized how unfair it all was.

"I… I've another plan," he murmured, taking Anders's hand. "It looks very busy here, and the service could be better. There is a small French restaurant just a bit farther down the Promenade. They also do very nice fish. So let's go there instead!"

Lise looked at him, a little surprised. She couldn't understand why he suddenly was so pale and tense, but she agreed.

"Do they have burgers?" Anders asked suspiciously.

"Yes, Anders. Burgers and ice cream. And their ice cream is much better than the hotel's."

The boy beamed at him, and they continued walking. Every step for Pierre was a pain, and he wondered if Sister Elena would recognize him from behind.

But no one came after him. No one called for him.

It was a reminder that the mundane happiness he had just experienced was a fragile illusion. Again he was aware of who he was, a man on the run from the law.

He didn't understand how he managed to finish the meal. It would have been unbearable if the little boy hadn't been with them. He chattered without hesitation, and Lise and Pierre sat quietly and listened.

Lise felt that something had happened. She saw that Pierre's eyes were dark with worry, and his hands trembled when he lifted the wineglass.

Afterward, he followed them up to Rue du Pont, and when they said goodbye outside the department store, he seemed to be in a hurry to leave them.

"And the bears?" said Anders as he stood with his hand in Pierre's. "Don't forget that you promised?"

Pierre shook his head. "No, Anders, I won't forget it. I'll talk with Mr. Cameron tonight and let you know on the beach tomorrow. Ok?"

He said the last thing to Lise. She looked at him seriously. He looked sick and torn as if consumed by an inner worry, and she felt sorry for him. Why was he so nervous? Maybe he already regretted his promise?

"You…you shouldn't feel obligated," said she in a low voice. "It doesn't matter if you want to postpone. We have the whole summer."

"Summer is short here," he replied and avoided her gaze. "No, Lise, we're going ahead with the hike. I'll meet you tomorrow at the same place on the beach, then I will have spoken to Mr. Cameron."

"Thanks for a nice day, Eric." She hesitated. She wanted to say something more but couldn't find the words. He looked downright sick, and she did not understand.

"It could have been nicer if I didn't…" he said softly. "I'm sorry."

Now he looked directly at her. His eyes were so unhappy that she wanted to take him in her arms and caress him calmly, as if he had been a little boy who needed comfort. But he was not a little boy. He was a grown man. She placed a hand on his arm.

”Goodbye,” he said, turning abruptly and went. She watched him walk away down the street and disappear around a corner. Suddenly she got a strong feeling that she would never see him again.

”What happened to Eric?” said Anders, looking up at her questioningly.

”I don’t know, darling,” she replied, taking his hand. ”I do not know.”

”He looked like he was sick. But he wasn’t sick when we were on the beach.”

No, Lise thought, puzzled. He wasn’t sick when we were out on the beach. The change came when they stood outside the Hotel L’Escale, and he abruptly decided to go to the French restaurant instead. Why did he change his mind? It seemed as if he had recognized someone at the restaurant—someone he’d rather not meet.

”But we’ll see him tomorrow,” continued Anders.

Yes, we will, she thought. But she wasn’t sure. She wasn’t sure at all.

And despite the day being full of sunshine, it felt as if dark clouds suddenly gathered on the horizon.

It was Mrs. Cameron who found him.

It was past ten in the evening, and for several hours she had been worried that Mr. Roy had not come home. She and her husband had come to like the quiet and withdrawn lodger. They had no children of their own, and somehow she felt like a mother to the earnest young man who smiled so rarely.

"I don't understand," she said to her husband when she got up from the couch to put the kettle on—again. "He never stays out this late in the evenings. You don't think something could have happened?"

Bernard Cameron shook his head.

"Don't worry, Mollie. Mr. Roy is an adult. He can take care of himself. He's probably out with a sweet girl."

Mollie snorted.

"He's not like that! No, I think something has happened. He left early this morning. What if he swam too far and drowned? Maybe we should call the police."

"You can't run and call the police for this kind of thing, Mollie. Don't worry; he will come."

Mrs. Cameron went to the window and looked out into the night. The stars twinkled in the sky, and suddenly she froze.

Someone was sitting on the stairs.

A dark, motionless figure huddled, hiding his face in his hands.

"Bernard," she whispered. "Someone is sitting on the stairs. I… I don't know…but it looks like Mr. Roy. He looks strange. Maybe he's sick."

He might have had too much to drink, thought Bernard and got up and went to his wife. Yes, a man was sitting on the stairs, but he could not determine if it was their guest or someone else in the dark.

Together they went to the front door, and Mr. Cameron opened it while his wife switched on the outside lamp above the door.

It was Eric Roy sitting on the stairs.

He did not react to the sudden light. He sat huddled together, peculiarly stiff and with his face bowed in hands. It seemed he slept, but when Mrs. Cameron cautiously advanced and took him by the shoulder, he moved slowly, rocking side to side.

"Mr. Roy," Mollie whispered. "Come in with us. You can't sit here all night. You'll catch a cold."

The man did not answer. She noticed he was shaking, and when she put her hand on his forehead burned out of fever.

"Oh, Bernard," she said, startled. "He is ill. Mr. Roy is sick; he has a fever. We have to help him to his bed and call for the doctor. It is very bad, Bernard."

With united forces, the old couple managed to get their guest on his feet, and some minutes later, they had tucked him into bed.

He hadn't uttered a word the whole time, just moved as if in a trance and looked at them with blank, vacant eyes. But when Mr. Cameron was to call for a doctor, he suddenly sat up and looked at him with wild eyes.

"Not the police," he whispered with strange intensity. "Not the police. Not sister Elena. I want Lise to come. Not the police."

The two spouses looked worriedly and wonderingly at each other. What did he mean?

He had sunk back down onto the pillow and was now lying with closed eyes. His face looked haggard and gauntlet, and his forehead was sweaty.

Mrs. Cameron stroked his hair as she nodded at her husband.

"No, Mr. Roy, we won't call the police. We need to call a doctor. You are sick and in need of care."

"Lise," he murmured.

Then, Mrs. Cameron noticed that he had lost consciousness.

❦

The doctor who came was old. He had been Cameron's family doctor for almost forty years. He knew all about colds, children's diseases, and reliable home remedies, but he was not very well versed in modern medicine, and he could not find any sign of an organic illness with Cameron's guest.

Pierre had woken up again from unconsciousness and lay restless in bed with a high fever. The doctor gave him a shot to calm his anxiety.

"I think it is a nervous breakdown," said the doctor when he sat with the Camerons for a cup of tea in the kitchen. "What do you know about him? Does he have any difficult experiences in his past?"

He looked at Mrs. Cameron over the edge of his cup. Mollie shook her head.

"He is an engineer from Washington D.C., said he had pneumonia and came here to recover and rest."

"Engineer?" The doctor raised an eyebrow. "Are you sure, Mrs. Cameron?"

"That's what he said." Mollie pressed her thin lips together. "And I have no reason to question that. Mr. Roy is honorable. I have always been good at judging people."

The old GP said nothing but was convinced Mrs. Cameron was mistaken. The sick man had not spoken as an engineer but rather as someone with medical training. In his delirious state, he used terms indicating he was a brain specialist. He had spoken of a nurse named sister Elena and given her orders. But everything had been very fragmented, and it could happen that his delirious mind just reflected some TV series he'd recently watched.

"Thank you for the tea," said the doctor and stood up. "It's late, and I have to go home. A man my age…"

He shrugged and laughed. "But don't you worry about the patient, Mrs. Cameron. He will rest peacefully tonight, and I'll stop by again in the morning." He took his bag. "It is a very peculiar case," he added as he walked towards the door. "Very peculiar. But like I said… He will be back and well in a few days."

"Are you going out again?" Beth's voice was shrill, and she looked up from her knitting with a disapproving expression when Lise and Anders came out on the porch.

Lise had cleared the table and kitchen after breakfast, it was past ten in the morning, and she had slept very bad.

She just wanted to get to the beach as soon as possible to meet Eric. To be sure that her concern had been without grounds and that he would show up as promised.

She was no longer comfortable in her mother-in-law's house. Beth had caused a terrible scene when they came home late after the disastrous dinner at the French restaurant. She had reprimanded Lise for not calling home and announcing that she intended to eat out, and she was, of course, right. But on the other hand, Lise did not want to be treated like a child, and she suddenly thought that the atmosphere in the house threatened to strangle her.

"Yes, we're going out," she said calmly as she helped Anders with his jacket. "I was going to do a little shopping first, and then we'll go to the beach. Anders needs to be in the fresh air as much as possible."

"We have fresh air here in the garden, too," Beth said curtly.

"It does him good to be by the lake," replied Lise. "And don't worry about lunch for us. I'll buy us something on the Promenade."

"Isn't that an unnecessary expense," replied the mother-in-law. "You must learn to be more careful with money, Lise. Especially since we don't know about you getting the payout from the insurance."

Lise looked at her quickly. So, that's what she thought now. Earlier, she was so confident that the insurance money was a given thing. But now…

"Bye," she said stiffly and took the bag with their swimwear. Anders had run ahead and was now waiting eagerly at the gate.

The whole morning, he had not spoken of anything but the bears and the hike that Eric would take him to.

"Are you coming home for dinner?" asked Beth. "Or are you going to meet that Mr. Roy again?"

"We will be home for dinner. I have already promised to help Ana with the dinner."

Lise turned and left. She felt her mother-in-law's stare on her back and felt a little bad for being so sharp. Maybe the old woman felt disappointed that she could not join them because of her disability.

But Lise wouldn't let pity stop her. She was going to the beach and meeting Eric.

He had come to matter a lot to her in some strange way.

She couldn't explain why, but she tried to convince herself that it was because he seemed to have a soft spot for Anders. The boy had blossomed in Eric's presence. Anders appeared to have recovered from the shock he received from his father's death.

"Do you think Eric is already on the beach and waiting for us?" asked Anders as he skipped and jumped at her side.

"I don't know," she said. "We have some errands in town first. We'll buy you a new pair of swimming trunks."

"Why?" said the boy with a moan.

"You only have one pair, and I don't want you to run around in wet trunks after swimming."

She took his hand in an attempt to calm herself. The visit to the store was just a pretext.

She was afraid to come too early to the beach and find that Eric had not arrived.

The sun had begun to sink in the west when Lise gave up. They could not wait any longer; he would not come.

She had known it all along, ever since he left them so quickly the night before.

The hours had dragged by, and Anders had been impossible with his questions.

"Won't he come soon, Mom? Why isn't he here? He said he should talk to the man about the bears. He promised."

"Maybe he's sick," she replied. "He will surely come tomorrow."

The boy had calmed down. He was playing at the water's edge, they swam and played in the water together a few times, but Anders was somehow not engaged; his mind was elsewhere. Several times he stood frozen, staring towards town as if he expected Eric to come walking and minute.

Once, they had seen a solitary figure in the distance, and she had been seized with excitement and joy.

There he was.

But the solitary figure had materialized as a schoolboy collecting shells, and they were both disappointed.

"I thought it was him!" the boy exclaimed. "I thought for sure it was him."

"Eric must be ill," she said, trying to convince herself as much as the boy. "We'll meet him later. He will not let us down."

At half past five, she packed up their things and took Anders by the hand. She blamed herself for not getting his phone number or even knowing at which B & B he stayed.

They stopped to get ice cream on the Promenade for Anders. It was a half-hearted attempt to make him forget his disappointment. But it did not really work. As they passed the Hotel L'Escale's restaurant, he said, "This is where it happened." He looked at the people sitting in the garden.

Lise stopped and looked at him. "What do you mean?" she said slowly.

"This is where Eric got so weird yesterday," replied the boy. "When he saw that lady."

"Which lady?" Lise's voice was tense. She had previously noted that the child was good at seeing the small things.

"There were three sitting at a table, and when Eric saw them, he looked as if he had seen a ghost." Anders licked the ice cream and behaved as if nothing really happened.

"Sitting… Is that lady sitting here today?" Lise asked cautiously, examining the summer guests relaxing in the garden.

Anders shook his head. "No, I can't see her. She had a white hat."

"Do you think the lady saw Eric?"

"No, I don't think so. He turned away quickly, and then we went to the other restaurant."

Lise nodded. That could be an explanation. She also had a feeling that it was something that Eric at the hotel garden had scared him.

But why?

Who was the woman in the white hat?

No one had sent her a message. No one had stopped by the house. He knew her name and where she lived, but he had made no effort to contact her.

The evening seemed endless to her.

She sat with Beth and the personal support worker Ana in the living room and stared blankly at the TV.

She had no idea what they had been watching when she left for bed.

She lay on her back looking at the dark ceiling and couldn't sleep. She listened to Anders's calm breathing in the next-door room, but she could not feel any calm.

She tried to think it all through—logically and level-headed.

It had been something strange with Eric from the very beginning.

Not that time when they met outside Laurier's in D.C. when he rescued Anders from the traffic. Then he had seemed normal and ordinary, a tall, handsome man with kind eyes and charming features.

She had never forgotten that meeting, and she was pleasantly surprised when he entered the compartment on the train.

But then she noticed that there was something strange about him. He seemed depressed and down. He behaved strangely when the conductor came to check their tickets, and he quickly turned away when he caught sight of the policeman at the bus station in Neuveville.

Was he a criminal? A man on the run from justice?

No, she couldn't believe that.

He was a man of great tenderness, a man with love. He couldn't possibly have done something criminal.

She closed her eyes to wipe away his image, but she kept seeing his face before her. The thick dark hair, the kind brown eyes that looked so sad, the prominent nose, and the trimmed beard.

And suddenly, she realized what she felt for him.

She knew why his absence made her so disappointed.

And that knowledge frightened her, for she had been burned by love before, and she had no desire to experience that again.

She turned on her side and buried her face in the pillow.

She must forget that a man named Eric Roy existed and had to erase him from her mind.

Pierre opened his eyes and looked around bewildered before he made out a familiar face.

"What happened?" he asked uncertainly.

"You have been ill, Mr. Roy. But you are better. We have been so worried about you." Mrs. Cameron leaned over the bed and smiled at him. "Doctor Aubert has taken care of you. He says you will soon be able to go to the lake again. The sun has been too hot to be out all day."

"Doctor Aubert?"

Pierre just noticed the other person in the room. A man in his seventies with white hair and rosy cheeks. The strange man, the doctor, nodded and smiled.

"It is entirely to Mrs. Cameron's credit you have done so well, Mr. Roy," he said. "She has hardly left your side."

"How long have I been lying like this? What happened?"

The old doctor came to the bed and checked his pulse out of old habit.

"You have been ill for more than a week. Mrs. Cameron found you on the front steps with a high fever and seemed unaware of your whereabouts. They called for me, and I must confess that I don't know what you had caught. The world is full of strange diseases, and an old country doctor doesn't have time to keep up with all the new findings. But I think you had some sort of nervous breakdown, a collapse that affected you physically. We talk about psychosomatic cases, and this was probably one." He laughed a deep rolling laugh. "At least you are better, and I have prescribed a strengthening cure for you. In a few days, you will be back on your feet."

More than a week, Pierre thought. And suddenly, he remembered: he had arranged a meeting with Lise and Anders by the lake. He had promised to arrange the hike for them, and had he not come. Did they know he had been ill?

He looked at Mrs. Cameron.

"Has…has someone asked for me while I was sick?" he said softly.

"No, no one, Mr. Roy," she replied, a little surprised. "Who would that be? I thought you didn't know anyone here."

"Lise Norrgard," he said slowly but regretted it the next second. He had seen how the old doctor winced.

"Do you mean Beth's daughter-in-law?" he asked. "How do you know her?"

"I met her on the train and the bus coming here," Pierre couldn't help but reply, or the doctor might become suspicious.

"Oh, well, the young woman and her little son." The doctor smiled. "She is a recent widow," he explained, turning to Mrs. Cameron. "She has come here to be with Beth during the summer. Her husband—Beth's only son—died in a plane crash. A very beautiful woman," he said, facing Pierre again. "Do you want me to tell her that you have been sick? I'm going there in a day or so to check on Beth."

"No, no, that's not… We do not know each other that… It was just that I played a bit with her boy by the lake, and she might wonder why I disappeared." He fell silent. He hoped that his explanation would subdue the old doctor's curiosity. "Just forget it, doctor."

Aubert nodded and stood for a moment watching his patient.

"Tell me something, Mr. Roy. Molly here—Mrs. Cameron—says you're an engineer. But I think you are an M.D. You were delirious and talked quite a bit. On several occasions, it sounded like you were in full swing with a complicated surgery."

Pierre lay motionless. He felt the fear flood his veins again, and he closed his eyes to avoid the other's gaze.

"That…it must have been pure dreams," he mumbled.

Doctor Aubert laughed. "Yes, I thought so. You have probably watched too many episodes of some medical tv series."

He turned and began to pack his bag.

"Everyone stares at the TV all the time," he said to Mrs. Cameron. "I don't even own a set, and I won't get one either. And now there are streaming things, Molly. Do you have that?"

Mrs. Cameron shook her head with a smile. "From what I understand, there is a new series about a doctor on the run from the police. The other day one of my patients asked me if I thought the doctor was innocent or not, but what do I know?"

Pierre lay motionless and listened to the old doctor. Did he suspect something? Maybe he had recognized him?

But he soon calmed down as the old man was finished and came to the bed.

"I have to go now, Mr. Roy. You should be grateful for choosing engineering instead of the medical profession. A doctor never has any free time."

He smiled.

"You can get up but should take it easy the first few days. You have been through difficult days and must allow your strength some time to return. Don't forget to take your pills."

He left, and Mrs. Cameron followed him down.

Pierre lay alone for a long time, staring up at the ceiling.

During his illness, he had been spared from the thoughts of the past, but now they came to life again, and he didn't know what to do.

Should he surrender to the police and take his punishment?

Should he leave Neuveville?

This place had suddenly become dangerous. If he stayed, he risked meeting sister Elena again, and then she might see him.

But he suddenly knew he had to take the risk.

He wanted to see Lise again and fulfill his promise to her and Anders.

Two days later, he felt strong enough to leave the house for a walk to the beach again.

He avoided the Promenade with its tourists and Hotel L'Escale's restaurant. It was lunchtime, and if nurse Elena was still in Neuveville, she was perhaps sitting in the garden with her friends for drinks or a meal, and this time she might see him as he passed by. She could even be staying at the hotel. It was a good hotel but not excessively expensive, and a nurse could surely afford to stay there for vacations.

Lake Sables was full of small sailboats cruising the warm winds, and the air echoed with laughter and joyful shouts, and far out came a speedboat with a water skier in tow.

The people's carelessness rubbed off on Pierre, and when he had passed the busy parts of the beach, he increased his pace. His anxiety about meeting Lise and Anders was replaced by a bubbling anticipation. Suddenly, he knew he was in love with the beautiful redhead with the kind green eyes and the quiet smile.

In love?

He stopped.

Yes, he could no longer deceit himself. He was in love with Lise Norrgard, and this feeling was something completely different from what he had felt for Clara. With Clara, it had been desire and lust, young bodies longing for each other, and the relief of satisfaction. But with Lise, it was something completely different. Something more profound and more real. She gave him peace and happiness; her sheer presence gave him a peace he had never felt before.

But—it could not be, it was impossible.

He was a man without a name, a man without a future. He couldn't allow himself such feelings for Lise. Instead, he must suppress them and cover them up at any cost.

A love affair between them would only lead to disaster.

He continued at a slower pace. The beach got rockier, and the trees closed as a compact wall along the small path. When he arrived at their secluded place on the beach, it was empty.

He walked over to the rock where Lise used to sit with her back to the sun-warmed stone and sat down in her place.

Had they stopped waiting for him?

Was she disappointed with him because he had not appeared on that day as promised?

He leaned against the rock, closed his eyes, and buried his hands in the sand. They would not come here again. He knew it. She must have thought he had just made empty promises and never intended to take them on that hike to the other side of the lake.

Suddenly he heard a shout. He jerked and opened his eyes.

They had come from the footpath through the forest. Lise was dressed in a yellow dress, carrying a basket in one hand and holding little Anders in the other.

"There he is, Mom!" he heard the boy call out with a bright, eager voice. "There he is. I knew that he would come again!"

The boy freed himself from his mother's grip and rushed towards Pierre with a happy shout. Pierre opened his arms, and the boy threw his arms around Pierre's neck and buried his face in his neck.

"You're here!" he whispered, squeezing tight around Pierre's neck. It looked like he might never release him, and Pierre was filled with immense tenderness.

"I'm here, Anders," he whispered back. "And I have news that I think will make you happy."

Lise had come up close and looked at Pierre, her eyes serious, but there was a blush on her cheeks.

"So you finally returned, Eric," she said slowly. "I gave up hope, but Anders persisted in believing you would return."

"I knew it," said the boy, hugging Pierre again. "I knew it. And now you'll never leave again. Right, Eric?"

"Yes," Pierre replied softly, avoiding Lise's glance. "I will never leave you again."

They sat beside each other with their backs against the rock. Anders left after hearing about the hike to the bears and the Indian camp. He had found a good climbing tree where he played Indian by himself.

Pierre looked at Lise's hand and the wedding ring that sparkled in the sunshine as she let the sand drizzle between her fingers.

"I'm sorry I couldn't make it that day," he said, "but I got sick. I have been in bed for over a week and had no way to let you know."

"Ill?" She looked at him, searching for clues; his face looked pale and tired. "What did you catch?"

"The doctor couldn't quite tell, but he thought it was some sort of nervous breakdown." He smiled weakly. "I got a high fever."

"A nervous breakdown?" she said. "But…you don't seem the type for a nervous fit, Eric."

　　　　　　　　　　　　　　MATILDA HART

"One knows so little about oneself," he muttered. "I was very tired and down when I got here. I tried a little too hard." He shrugged his shoulders. "Let's not talk about me. Was your mother-in-law very angry when you came late that evening?"

Lise's eyes darkened. "She was furious. And I lost my cool. But it's better now," she added. "Sometimes it's better to say what you really think. To clear the air... she is a rather selfish woman, my mother-in-law. She has lived alone, bound to her wheelchair, and perhaps one shouldn't judge her by the same standards you use for others."

Their hands touched, but Lise yanked away her hand and placed it in her lap. The light touch had made her strangely upset; her whole body burned. Her heart filled with happiness at his return, she had missed him more than she wanted to admit, and her disappointment and sorrow had grown for each day they came to the beach without finding him. But now he was back. They sat close together. She could smell his discrete aftershave and the warmth of his body.

"Do you still miss your husband as much as...in the very beginning?" he said slowly.

She didn't look at him but started to draw incomprehensible figures in the sand with her finger.

"I have never missed my husband, Eric," she said with a whisper. "You might think I'm weird saying such a thing, but relief was my only feeling after the first shock of the disaster had subsided."

"Relief?" He looked at her in surprise. "But I thought you were happy. You said that your husband and Anders—"

"A son and a wife do not always feel the same things. Once upon a time—when we were newlyweds—I was very much in love with Michael. I adored him with stormy naive love, but after a few months of marriage, I discovered he cheated on me. There was a secretary at the office, and someone sent me an anonymous text telling me…"

She sat quietly for a moment, and he kindly interjected, "You don't have to tell me all this, Lise. I see that it hurts."

"No." She shook her head, and the copper curls glistened in the sun. "No, I want to tell you, Eric. I've never told anyone before, and my mother-in-law has no idea what it was like between her son and me. I want you to know." She searched for words and continued after a moment of silence. "I showed Michael that text when he came home over a weekend, but he just laughed at me. 'Are you so stupid that you think I can settle for just one woman?', he said. 'There is a lot of stress in my work. I need to relax after a day of tough international negotiations'. And I was to understand and accept that this was common in his profession and meant nothing. But I couldn't take it. That was too far from everything I was raised to respect, and I could not accept it."

"But I was pregnant and in a foreign country. Anders was born six months later, and I didn't have the courage to leave Michael. I remained in the marriage and, for our son's sake, for five long years…" She closed her eyes, and her hand with the large wedding band lay still on the sand. "And then…the accident happened. And all I could feel was relief."

He looked at her in silence. He wanted to put his arm around her and pull her close, but her next words filled his veins with ice.

"You see, Eric, I could never live a lie again. I imagined that it really was a difference between us and that Michael actually needed those women to vent the tension that must, after all, be in his profession, but in the end, I understood that it was not right. He had lied. And lies cannot exist between two people who really love each other. Michael lied, and I felt I was slowly dying in the relationship. So I must have the truth. I cannot live without truth, and a couple must share the same truth."

He turned away and looked over the glittering water. It was as if the sun had suddenly lost all warmth, and he wanted to run away.

He knew that what she said was honest and true. She was no woman who could live with a lie, and he was just one big lie. Eric Roy or Pierre Lyon-Cote, or both.

He was caught in his own net, and there was no escape. It was too late. He had promised them the hike and would deliver on his promise. Then, after they returned, he would leave. He would leave Neuveville and go to some distant place where no one cared about Eric Roy, and no Lise and Anders would suffer for his mere existence.

"I…I think I have to go back now," he muttered. "I'm still weak after the illness. But I will sort everything with old Cameron and let you know when."

"What should we pack?" she said in a lighter voice.

"Normal hiking stuff. Good shoes, warm clothes, a change or two, and stuff like that." He shrugged. "It will be rather primitive, but the camp is stored with most things we'll need. Bring something you can sleep in. We will use sleeping bags and probably share the same tent."

He didn't look at her, but he heard her giggle.

"What is it, Eric? Are you too shy to share a tent with me?"

He still wasn't meeting her gaze.

"I have to go now," he repeated.

He dared not show her his face, fearing that she would read all his feelings. But as he rose, she got up too.

"Then we'll go too," she said calmly. "I do not want you to go alone. I feel a responsibility for you."

Now he looked at her.

Her eyes were bright and kind, her face serious, but then she smiled.

"By the way, it's just selfishness," she said. "I don't want to miss that hike for all the money in the world."

And then she turned and called to the boy who sat on a branch in the tree.

❤

They parted on Rue du Pont, as usual. He stood and looked after them for a long time. Anders turned again and again and waved at him.

It was five o'clock, and the main street was busy. The crowd soon swallowed the tall, slim redhead and the little boy, and Pierre turned to go home. Then an electric shock shot through his body.

A woman was walking down the other side of the street. He caught only a glimpse of her profile, but he immediately recognized her.

She was wearing a white dress that was provocative at best with its short hemline and deep cleavage. Just the kind of dress a woman like that would wear in the summer, just as tall and voluptuous as when he and Peter Dahl spoke to her.

Latonya Williams from the makeshift bar in the abandoned Lock house by the Canal.

She had promised to testify in Pierre's favor. She had promised to testify in court that Julio Alvarado was highly intoxicated the night Pierre hit him on the Interstate.

Her testimony would have cleared Pierre completely. No judge in the world would have sentenced him to such a severe punishment if there was reason to suspect that the person hit was responsible for the accident.

But Latonya Williams had never appeared in court, and when they started looking for her, they found out that she had packed up her stuff and moved out of town. She had left no traces, and Pierre and his lawyer were convinced that her departure had been arranged. That the prosecutor, in some way, was behind it because they wanted to make an example of Pierre at any cost.

They couldn't prove it, of course. And his lawyer hadn't even mentioned Latonya Williams in the defense. She had considered it would hurt their case if they tried to cast suspicion on the prosecution, and she was probably right.

But on Rue de Pont in Neuveville, of all places, Latonya Williams walked proudly with swaying hips and a cheeky smile on her full lips.

She could still get him free.

If he could get her to sign a testimony that Alvarado was drunk that evening. Pierre didn't know if such testimony would clear him, but it was possible.

His case was pending before the Department of Justice on Pennsylvania Avenue. If the attorney general had such testimony, there was a good chance that he would annul the previous conviction.

He was about to cross the street when the traffic started moving again as the lights switched to green.

He started running down the sidewalk.

All the while, he tried to keep the black curly head in sight. He couldn't afford to lose her. She was his only chance. She was life for him.

Just as he got a chance to cross the street, she disappeared.

She had entered through the sliding doors of the department store, and desperation shot up inside him.

He had to find her.

He must make her talk.

It was his life—and his and Lise's life.

When he had crossed the street and entered the department store, he stopped inside the doors. It was huge, a concrete giant, several stories high, with lifts, escalators, and various aisles.

He had to find her.

His gaze searched the various counters and spaces between them. There were lots of women. But nowhere

did he see Latonya Williams, the hostess of the illegal
bar by the Chesapeake and Ohio Canal.

The department store was crowded. People pushed and shoved as the summer season sale was in full bloom.

Pierre's courage sank.

How would he find Latonya Williams in all this mess?

And then he caught sight of her again.

She was on the escalator going up, and for a moment, he thought she looked straight at him. But she did not recognize or see him; the second after, she was gone.

The way to the escalator appeared blocked by the shoppers, and Pierre had to push into one of the lifts instead.

He had to get hold of her, a word from her, and he would be a free man.

In the lift, he wondered which department a woman like Latonya Williams would visit. The opportunities were nearly infinite, but he went for the women's clothes department on the third floor by chance.

This floor was less crowded than the ground floor. A young woman with a tired face made no attempt to assist anyone.

He had guessed right.

Latonya Williams stood by one of the displays showing colorful beachwear. She was alone, and he slowly approached her and lay his hand on her shoulder.

"Ms. Williams?" he said. "Do you remember me?"

She spun and was a little startled. Her beautiful face looked very young and vulnerable for a moment. Not even the thick makeup and the bush of hair could hide the stupidity in her eyes. She looked like she wanted to escape most of all, and he understood that she recognized him.

"Do you remember that night at your makeshift bar?" Pierre continued softly. "You promised to appear in court and testify that Julio Alvarado was drunk on the night he was killed. Don't you remember that?"

She didn't answer. Her big dark brown eyes stared at him, and he saw fear in them.

He took her by the arm.

"Don't you remember your promise? Why didn't you come? Why did you leave Washington D.C.?"

She shook her head. Her face closed up, and her red lips shut hard.

"What do you say, Ms. Williams?" he said. "I wish you no harm. I just want you to sign a testimony in which you explain that Alvarado was drunk. If you just do that, I promise to leave you alone. No harm will come to you."

In a sudden unexpected move, she tore herself free from his grip.

"What do you do?" she almost screamed. "What are you talking about? I don't know of any bar. I have never heard the name, Julio Alvarado. I have never seen you before!"

"But…" said Pierre, startled. "You must recognize me? I am Dr. Lyon-Cote, Doctor Pierre Lyon-Cote from Washington D.C. My friend and I came down to you at the bar by the Canal. You served us foul drinks. You told us about Alvarado's visit and how drunk he was. You promised to testify."

A man in a black uniform came up to them, looking questioningly from Latonya Williams to Pierre.

"Everything right here?" he said.

Relief flashed over the woman's face. "This man molested me," she said, nodding at Pierre. "He says the craziest things. Can't one be left in peace at your department store?"

Her eyes sparkled with anger.

"Do you want us to call the police, madame?" said the department store guard.

"Do not bother," Latonya Williams hissed. "I don't intend to buy anything in a place where you cannot look at items without being harassed by strange men!"

She jerked her head. With an offended look, she pushed out her bosom and wiggled to the escalators. Even in her agitated state, she did not forget her seductive stride, and when she disappeared, Pierre knew he had lost his last chance.

Latonya Williams had recognized him. She had known who he was and what he was talking about. But she wasn't going to help. The prosecution in Washington D.C. had done their job well. Maybe they had paid her or held something over her head, but they had obviously frightened her, so she no longer intended to do anything for Pierre.

"What was that about?" said the security guard with an aggressive look.

Pierre shrugged. "I was wrong. I am sorry, but I was wrong. It was not my intention to scare your customers. I just thought she looked like someone I knew once…a long time ago."

As he walked to the stairs, he felt that everything that happened in Washington D.C. was a hundred years ago. The life he lived before he became Eric Roy would never come back. He was on the run, and there was no turning back.

He would fulfill his promise to Lise and Anders, and when they returned from their excursion, he would leave them and never see them again.

He could no longer stay in Neuveville.

Latonya Williams had recognized him.

She knew he was Pierre Lyon-Cote, a man who was on the run from the law.

She could suddenly get the idea to tell the police where he was to get him out of her hair.

The phone call came just after eight on Thursday evening. Beth was resting because the pain in her leg was worse than usual, and the intense ringtone woke her up.

She looked a little surprised at the phone Lise had left on the table. Who was it? No one she knew would call this late.

With a small moan, she sat up and looked at the display. It showed a man's name. Eric.

Beth flinched. It was him. The enemy. The strange man Anders had so fondly told her about. The man who had played with him by the lake. The man who seemed to have taken Michael's place in her grandson's life, the man who made Lise's cheeks blush.

Her first thought was to reject the call, but Lise would, sooner or later, find out, and then she would think even less about her mother-in-law.

She called out to Lise that her phone was ringing.

Lise rushed in, their eyes met, and Lise blushed as she picked it up and answered.

"Yes, hello, Eric. It's me." She fell silent and covered the microphone.

"I'll talk outside," she said to her mother-in-law. "I don't want to bother you. You had almost fallen asleep."

"But I'm awake now. You woke me," Beth answered with self-pity.

Lise hesitated, then removed her hand from the device and listened. She didn't look at her mother-in-law, but she knew Beth's eyes followed every change in her countenance.

"Sure," she said. "That will be good. Half past eight the day after tomorrow, at pier three. And the boat is called Wet Lady?" She laughed. "What a name. And you will be there?"

She nodded eagerly, and Beth noted that her eyes sparkled.

"Do we need more than warm clothes and toiletries? No food?"

The man said something that Beth could not hear. But she saw that Lise's smile deepened, and her eyes were filled with a dreamy expression.

"Nice," her daughter-in-law said. "We will be there. Anders is already in bed, but he will be delighted when I tell him in the morning. See you on Saturday then.

Half past eight. Pier three. We will be there, Eric. And, Eric…it will be wonderful."

She slowly hung up. She had forgotten her mother-in-law's presence for a brief moment, but then she gathered herself with a pale smile.

"I'm sorry you were disturbed," she said. "I will not place my cell on the table again. I'll leave you to rest now."

Beth shook her head and kept her eyes on Lise.

"Who is he?" she asked sharply.

"Mr. Roy from Washington D.C., that man I told you about."

"And what did he want?"

"He has offered Anders and me to hike across the lake to see the bear and the Indian camp. We'll stay for a few days, which will be a great experience for Anders."

"A hike?" said Beth. "But…that's ridiculous. It's very primitive, and you are to share a tent with that man. What does he really want from you?"

Lise hesitated, then looked directly at her mother-in-law.

"He doesn't want anything from me, Beth," she said. "He is just a good friend, a man who has had some difficulties. He was sick recently, but now he is well again and doing this for Anders's sake."

"And you want me to believe that?" Beth snorted in a mocking accusation.

"You can believe what you want," Lise answered, heading for the door.

"But…you don't know him at all. He could be anyone. A scoundrel, a swindler. Anyone. His very name—Eric Roy—sounds fake."

Lise turned in the doorway. She looked at the old woman that half lay against the pillows on the couch, and her eyes were completely calm.

"There is nothing fake about Eric Roy," she said softly. "He is a very good person. And he is good for Anders. He's almost made the boy forget what happened, and for that, I am very thankful."

"You know nothing about him. And yet you plan to hike with him for several days and nights."

"You forget that Anders is there," Lise replied. "And you also forget I no longer have a husband to answer to. I'm free, Beth. And I do what I want. Good night."

She turned and left, and Beth could hear her heels move toward the stairs.

The old woman sank back against the pillow. She was perhaps restricted in her movements, shackled to a wheelchair and a bed, dependent on other people's help. But she had a phone beside her, and she could still contact anyone in the outside world.

She decided to call old Doctor Aubert the next day.

Lise had said that Eric Roy had been ill. It may have been Dr. Aubert who looked after him. And if that was the case, she would surely be able to find out more details about the mysterious Mr. Roy from Washington D.C. Doctor Aubert knew where to look and noticed things; besides, he had been her family's doctor and friend for many years. If he knew anything about Lise's friend, he would tell her.

Beth intuitively felt that something was peculiar with Eric Roy.

And he was about to take the apple of her eye, her only grandchild, from her, and that would not happen if she could stop it.

Not at any price.

Like the other smaller boats, the *Wet Lady* lay by Pier Three and jerked and tore at the mooring ropes.

It was an old motorboat with a small deck house that Bernard Cameron had bought secondhand, but he loved her and looked after her like a precious princess. The winters were long at Lake Sable, and only during a few short summer months could one enjoy a boat. Bernard started preparing the Wet Lady for the season as the first buds of spring flowers pushed up through the snow.

He bent over the gas tank and checked there was enough petrol for the trip across the lake and back when he heard Eric Roy call for someone on the pier. When he looked up, he saw the woman who would come with them, the woman and her little son.

He also saw Mr. Roy going to meet them, almost with hesitation. Bernard's old eyes were still good: he noticed that Mr. Roy was different than he had been just a few minutes ago when he helped stow rations in the boat.

The tall man suddenly looked like one young boy, and he had a slight blush under the tan as he extended his hand in greeting the woman.

And Bernard understood. The woman was very beautiful. She was wearing long green slacks and a loose white sweater, but the water's light wind made the shirt cling to her body and revealed that she was very shapely.

The copper-red hair hung loose over her shoulders, and her eyes sparkled as she looked up at Eric Roy.

Bernard smiled. He knew what that meant. Mr. Roy was in love but didn't want to admit he was. But, on the contrary, it looked as if he tried to hide it at all costs, both from himself and for her.

A few days in the quiet forest, maybe mother nature would solve all the problems, thought Bernard, scratching his neck. The wilderness had a rare ability to get people to come to terms with their inner thoughts, and these two looked as if they were determined for each other.

"Are you the captain?" he heard a young voice beside him, and he noticed the boy standing next to the boat. The boy's eyes were big and blue, and his face beamed with anticipation.

Bernard nodded. "Are you perhaps afraid to come aboard?" he said with a twinkle in his eye.

"Afraid!" the boy exclaimed and climbed onboard. "I am never afraid. I just want to know if you will let me steer the boat?"

"Well, you'll have to stand on a box. Otherwise, you won't see over the edge." Bernard grinned.

"Oh, can I?" The boy began to jump up and down, but Bernard shook his head.

"In that case, you must first learn to keep calm because the sea can be quite rough out there, and I don't want my passengers falling overboard."

The boy instantly became still, and his gaze serious. "I promise," he said.

Bernard smiled and ruffled his hair. "That's much better," he muttered. "You are a good boy. And you seem very sensible for your age."

He turned around. The woman had come down to the boat, and he held out his hand to assist her onboard.

"Good day, Mr. Cameron," she said. "I'm Lise Norrgard. It is terribly kind of you to take us across the lake."

Bernard blinked. Up close, she was even more beautiful than he initially thought. There was something calm and proud about her revealed balance and inner strength. And he hoped that Mr. Roy would get his feelings straight and dare to tell her about it. She was just the type he needed, someone to rid the concern from his eyes.

"It was entirely Mr. Roy's doing," Bernard mumbled and added after a moment's silence, "I hope you will take good care of him, Mrs. Norrgard. Out there in the forest. He needs it. He is a very lonely man."

Lise looked at him, a little surprised. Then she smiled and nodded. Here was another person who cared a lot for Eric.

"I will do my best," she said softly while the tall man on the dock untied the moorings and jumped aboard.

Her heart seemed to have turned into a ball of nerves when she thought of spending time with Eric, being close to him for several days.

She heard the old man start the engine, and Eric came to her and stood beside her at the railing.

"How do you feel?" he said.

"Like being freed," she replied, looking towards the Promenade and the green roof of Hotel L'Escale.

She thought of Beth.

❤

When they set up camp for the night, it was almost dark. They had eaten a late lunch as they reached the shore on the other side of the lake and then walked for hours. Lise carried most of their pack, and Pierre carried Anders, who became too tired to walk and had fallen asleep as they reached the spot for the first night's camp.

They helped set up the tent, and Lise placed Anders within without waking him.

"Should I make us something to eat?" asked Lise as she came out from the tent.

Pierre shook his head.

"It is late, and I believe the young man will wake early, don't you?"

She smiled. He was so right.

They brushed their teeth and got ready for the night, and when he came into the tent, she was already lying in her sleeping bag. But her eyes twinkled at him, and she smiled.

"I'm so happy," she whispered. "It feels completely unreal, but I'm so grateful you brought us here, Eric."

"It's good," he murmured. "We shall have some days of total freedom. Up here, we can forget everything that lies behind us."

She nodded as he crawled into his sleeping bag.

"It already feels like I've started a new life," she said. Soon after, she fell silent, and when Pierre turned to look at her, she lay with her eyes closed. She slept.

A new life, he thought, looking into the dark, and he wished he could believe in a new life for himself, forgetting everything that lay behind him.

But in the dark, he thought he saw a series of faces.

Judge Kavanaugh staring at him with hard, hostile eyes.

Josef Espina, the prosecutor, pointed a finger at him.

The hateful look from Alvarado's widow.

Clara, stiff and closed on the audience bench.

Peter and Astrid Dahl…

He shivered. The night was suddenly cold and hostile, and he felt ashamed of himself for the first time since this all started.

He listened to Lise's and the boy's calm breathing and wished he had never met them.

He loved them.

He loved Anders as if the boy was his own, and he loved the quiet, beautiful woman who trustingly had followed him here.

She had no idea that Eric Roy was a simple criminal, a man with a false name, who told her lies about himself, and suddenly he was afraid of what this would lead to.

"I must leave them as soon as we return to Neuveville," he said to himself.

But he didn't know if he would have the strength to do it.

So he closed his eyes and listened to the sounds around him. In the silence of the night, he heard the wind in tall tall trees, an owl screeching far away, the anxious beating of his own heart, and then he fell asleep.

Lise woke up with a jolt. At first, she had no idea where she was, it was dark, and the air was filled with peculiar scents. Scents of trees and grass.

And then she remembered.

She was not in the old guest bed in her mother-in-law's house but in a tent in the forest.

Then she heard the sound that had woken her again. It came out of the darkness, but it wasn't Anders who cried. He slept deeply beside her, wrapped, or rather tangled, in his sleeping bag.

The wailing grew, and she understood that it had to be Eric. The faint sound was full of torment. It scared her and filled her with compassion at the same time.

She crawled out of the sleeping bag and made her way to the other side of the tent where he slept. She could just make out his face in the soft darkness.

He slept. His face was at peace, but occasionally a muscle under his left eye twitched, and he uttered sounds.

She could make out some words: "I don't want...I'm free, innocent. Clara...help me..."

His whole body jerked, but he did not wake. Apparently, he was dreaming, but it wasn't a pleasant dream.

She gently stroked her fingers over his forehead, he was hot and damp with sweat, and she remembered that he had recently been ill. He had said something about a nervous breakdown, but why would a man like Eric have a nervous breakdown? He was strong, he looked healthy, and he seemed to be entirely in tune with himself.

Or was he?

She looked at his face and realized she knew very little about him. Her mother-in-law's suspicious words came to her: *Eric Roy…sounds fake…*

Beth had been right. Eric Roy was such a common and insignificant name that it was difficult to connect it to this man.

He had said he lived in D.C. and was an engineer, and he had taken a leave to recover from severe pneumonia earlier in the year.

All of that could be true, but it could also be made up.

He had never supplied her with any details of his life; only once had he become more emotionally engaged. That was when he told about his childhood at Lake Sables. His parents had died when he was the same age as Anders, but he remembered them quite clearly. He had been cared for by relatives, and this was the first time since childhood that he revisited Neuveville. He had told about the Indian princess his grandfather married— her name had been; it was a beautiful name, filled with poetry, and it meant "she who speaks to them."

He could also speak to them. When he was with Anders, she noticed a spark in his friendly eyes; and when she smiled at him.

When she looked at his face, he looked naked, young, and a little sad.

I don't care who he is, she thought and stroked his forehead again.

"Pierre," he murmured. "Pierre Lyon-Cote…and Clara…"

Lise wondered who Clara was, and a wave of jealousy splashed over her when she realized how little she knew about his past. But she didn't care if his name was Eric Roy or something else…for her, he was a person full of kindness to her and her son when they were having a hard time, and she did not want to take that away from him.

He had made Anders happy again. The boy seemed to have forgotten the terrible things about Michael's death. Anders had embraced Eric as strongly and spontaneously as he had loved his father.

And what about her?

Something purred inside her as she looked down at the sleeping man. He gave her peace, but he also gave her much worry. But it was a worry that Michael, her late husband, had never been able to wake up in her, not even during their most joyful times.

A sweet worry, she thought, smiling to herself. *I don't know what it can lead to, and it's too early to think about that, but there is nothing to this man that can give me fear. Just a sweet worry…*

He slept silently now. His breaths were calm and even. The nightmare had disappeared as quickly as it arrived.

"I don't want you to have nightmares, my love," she whispered, suddenly taken aback as she formed those words. "My love…"

She sat still for a moment, almost bewildered, then bent down over the sleeping man and kissed him lightly on the mouth.

He didn't wake up, but she saw a smile flash over his lips.

When she carefully zipped her own sleeping bag to go back to sleep, she didn't understand what she'd done.

She had acted like a romantic schoolgirl.

She should be furious with herself.

But, it was as if something deep inside her body sang, cheered, and bubbled from expectations.

A sweet worry, she thought. *A sweet worry, but no fear.*

It was a three hour walk to the ranger's camp. Anders led the way, pointing at bushes, flowers, butterflies, and anything else he found interesting.

Pierre and Lise followed; now and then, they touched hands, and she noticed that he withdrew with a flinch every time.

"You are so quiet, Eric," she said. "Are you still bothered by that nightmare you had last night?"

He stopped and glared at her. "Nightmare?"

She nodded and smiled.

"You woke me up. You seemed to have a bad one. You talked loudly and said a lot of incomprehensible things."

"What did I say?" His voice was strained.

Lise shook her head. "There was no meaning in it, just words. But I understood that you were very upset."

He continued walking, fixing his gaze on the happy boy in front of them.

"Did I mention any names, Lise?" he said in a whisper.

"You talked about a Clara." She fell silent. She didn't want to ask too much. She was convinced that someday, he would tell her everything.

"Clara?" He stopped again and looked at her. "Nothing more?"

"And a man's name…Pierre Lyon-Cote," she hesitated. Somehow, she felt she was treading dangerous grounds, and she didn't want to ruin this bright and happy day.

"That…those are people I knew once," he said softly. "They mean nothing anymore. I can't understand why I dreamt about them," he added fiercely and started walking again.

Anders ran back to them and eagerly pointed to something farther along the path between the tall fir trees.

"Mom! Eric! It's the camp! It's the ranger's camp!"

The rugged narrow path under the tall larches and firs opened up to reveal the camp of the Park Rangers.

A few curious tourists silently stared at them as they walked into the open place surrounded by traditional log cabins. An old man with a weathered face and wearing a leather hat walked slowly towards them.

"Welcome," he said. "Welcome to Monts-la-Croix National Park; I am Tom, your guide for this visit."

"Thank you," Pierre replied, shaking the man's outstretched hand. "I am Eric Roy, and this is Lise Norrgard and her son Anders."

"Nice meeting you all," he said with a smile that softened the rugged, tanned, and weathered features. "Anders, that sounds Scandinavian to me. You're from Sweden?" He peered at the boy.

"No," he replied. "Mom is from Denmark, Dad is from Canada, and I live in America, but now we live here…" His voice trailed off, and he looked down on the sandy ground.

"If you are hungry, there are fresh bannocks for you. Arriving visitors usually want bannocks."

They gladly accepted this offer, and Anders was delighted with the warm flatbread served directly from the hot stone.

"Would you prefer your own tent, or would you like to try our guest cabin?" Tom asked.

"Mom!" Anders almost cried. "Mom, can we sleep in the cabin like the rangers? Please!"

Lise smiled and looked at Pierre with a mix of questioning and pleading.

"Of course," he said with a broad smile. "Of course, we can stay in the cabin."

Anders jumped joyfully, and Tom showed them to the cabin on the outskirts of the camp. It smelled heavily of fresh wood, a small fire was burning in the iron stove, and the smell of burning logs felt very homely. It was warm and dimly lit.

"This will be your quarters. We have aired the mattresses in your beds," said Tom, pointing to the two bunk beds.

"There is a stream just behind the camp where you can wash. Tomorrow I will take you on a hike, and maybe we will see some bears." He looked at the boy with a mischievous smile.

"Look, Mom!" Anders almost shouted as they walked the forest trail the next day. "Look up there in the tree!"

"Is it a bear?" asked Pierre with a smile.

Anders shook his head.

"Tom told me it's a porcupine, a Canadian porcupine. They are not dangerous. They climb to the treetops and hang there to be left in peace. You can eat them, he says, but you never hunt them."

"Yes, they say they are the hunter's last chance," Pierre added.

"The hunter's last chance?" Lise looked up at the animal curled into a big furry ball.

"That is what they say," said Pierre. "They are very slow, and if a hunter got lost in the wasteland and ran out of ammunition, he could always survive by catching a porcupine. They have saved many lost men, and you don't kill them if not really necessary."

"You know quite a lot, coming from D.C. How do you know so much about the animals in the vast forests, Eric?"

Lise looked at him wide-eyed.

A shadow passed over his face.

"You forget I was born up here," he muttered. "I was raised by relatives who lived rather isolated, and during my holidays, I roamed a lot in the forests. But then…" He shrugged his shoulders. They took a moment and studied the peculiar animal.

They came to a high barren rock with a magnificent view over the whole park.

"It feels like standing on top of the world," whispered Lise, squeezing Anders's hand.

"Tom said we might spot bears down there," said the boy.

She hoped he wouldn't be too disappointed if they didn't see any bears. A porcupine was good enough for her; she was more than happy with the tranquil freedom of the forest—and the company.

They sat down to eat the provisions they had brought, enjoying the lovely weather, the warm breeze, and the peaceful moment.

Tom ate nothing and sat on the side, smoking a cigarette, not wanting to bother the others. But she sat down by him.

"Have you been here long, Tom?" Lise asked.

The man shook his head.

"I don't know," he said. "What do you mean by long? If I asked the Indians, they might think long is a few hundred years, and for a New Yorker, it's two days." He laughed short.

Lise had a whim.

"Do you remember a family called Lyon-Cote?" she said lightly.

"Lyon-Cote?" The Ranger's creased face was impossible to read, but he nodded slowly and thoughtfully.

"It was long ago, just as I came to work here. I remember some accident in Neuveville…"

Lise hesitated and looked at Pierre. He and Anders sat some distance from them. They talked and pointed at different things in the distance, and he did not seem to listen to her conversation.

"Do you know what happened?" she said softly.

Tom shook his head.

"It was some accident where two people died. Parents, I think, and they left a child that was taken in by child care, or was it, relatives?"

"You… you don't know what the family's name was?" Lise looked at the Ranger. "Maybe their name was Roy?"

"I don't know. I cannot remember, but there should be records at City Hall if you really want to know."

She nodded in silence. Had Eric Roy's ancestors changed his name as they took him in? She stood up and walked over to him. He was still looking out over the surrounding forest and distant lake. Although he seemed totally lost in thought, she knew he was aware of her presence.

She intended to talk to him about what Tom had said, but she couldn't. Instinctively she felt that she shouldn't do that. Instead, she said softly, "Are you happy, Eric? Just as happy as I am?"

He turned to her and looked at her. Then he smiled—a forced and almost sad smile.

"Yes, Lise, right now I'm very happy."

But she knew that wasn't true. Something troubled him, and he would never be completely happy until he was free from that burden.

They sat on the small porch of the log cabin in the twilight. It had been four days since they left, and tomorrow they would return to Neuveville. Mr. Cameron was to pick them up at the jetty where he left them a few days ago.

"It's been absolutely amazing, Eric," said Lise. "Whatever happens later, I will always treasure these days."

He sat in silence. The scent of the trees, the grass and leaves, and the ever-burning log fires filled her with melancholy, and she suddenly felt like crying. The summer slipped away so fast, and nothing decisive came from it.

One day when they had been washing up at the stream, she had imagined something would happen. She had tripped over a branch when she got out of the water, and Eric, who was right behind her, had caught her. His delicate hands had fondled her breasts for a moment, and he had pressed her body close to his wet bare chest. At that moment, she had expected a kiss. She had wanted a kiss. She didn't care what else happened. Her body was filled with a fierce longing for him that it almost hurt.

But he had immediately released her and turned away as if ashamed of what had happened.

She was deeply disappointed at that moment, and she knew he understood her feelings. But they hadn't said anything, and soon after, they returned to the camp where Anders was playing with other visitors' children.

"I will never forget these days, Lise," Pierre said softly. "I'm sorry if everything did not turn out exactly as you wished."

He didn't look at her, but she understood that he had somehow guessed her thoughts.

A sudden frustration and anger flared up within her.

"What do you know about my wishes?" she exclaimed. "What do you really know about any woman, Eric? Are you a man of flesh and blood or…" She bit her lip. She had gone too far and regretted her words when she saw his miserable look.

"Please, forgive me, Eric." She stretched out her hand and placed it on his thigh.

He slowly shook his head.

"You have nothing to ask forgiveness for, Lise. On the contrary, it is you who…"

He never finished the sentence as Ranger Tom suddenly stood before them.

"Yes, Tom"? Pierre said softly, looking up at the Ranger. "What is it?"

"One of the visiting women is ill. We have tried to give her some painkillers, but it did not help. Do you have any medical skills, Mr. Roy?"

"I'm coming. I will come right away." He stood up so quickly that Lise's hand was thrown from his lap, but he didn't notice. It was as if all the doubt, insecurity, and lack of energy left him in a flash. She saw a new Eric Roy. A man of strong will and great determination.

She followed the two men to another guest cabin. Her eyes had difficulty adjusting to the darkness inside, but after a while, she saw that Eric was kneeling next to a bed with a silently wailing woman.

Eric examined the sick woman. Lise regarded him with rising wonder. His hands moved so easily over the woman's body. It looked like he knew what he was doing, but Eric wasn't a physician; he was an engineer…and what did an engineer know about medicine?

The sick woman's body contracted as if in a convulsion when Eric pressed his finger to her stomach, and soon after, he rose and turned.

"She needs to go to the hospital immediately. Appendicitis. Her appendix has ruptured, and she will die if not treated."

Tom dialed the emergency number, explained the situation, and then turned back to Eric.

"They will send a helicopter."

Eric nodded.

"That's good," he said. He bent over the woman and took her pulse. He looked at Tom.

Lise and Eric remained with the sick woman until the men from the emergency helicopter came in with a stretcher and carried her away. It was late, but the summer nights were not dark in these parts. The air felt like blue velvet against her face, and she was full of wonder.

"How did you know it was appendicitis, Eric?" she said as they went to bed. "You're not a doctor."

He looked at her quickly, then shrugged and held back the curtain.

"I have had appendicitis," he replied. "I remember it just like that. It will be fine as soon as she's in the hospital. There are excellent doctors there."

Wet Lady was already at the jetty when they arrived the following day. Bernard Cameron waved at them.

"You look like a real trapper," he said and grinned at Anders, whose face had turned copper by the sun.

"I *am* a trapper," answered the boy. "Tom showed me how to trap rats, and we saw a porcupine!"

Cameron shook his head to indicate how impressed he was. "Then I have to tuck in my tail."

Lise and Pierre looked at each other. They laughed, but their eyes were serious. The outing was over. The summer was ending, and it would never come back. Right now, at the end of July, there was already a chill in the wind that came from the mountains, and soon it would be all over.

Pierre stood next to Cameron when the boat backed out from land. The old man's hands rested safely on the steering wheel, and because of the engine noise, Lise could not hear what they were talking about.

"You look sad, Mom," she heard Anders say.

He came over to her and curled up next to her on the bench, and she put her arm around his slim shoulders and pulled him tightly to her.

"You're trembling. Are you cold?"

"No, Anders, I'm not cold. Maybe I'm just kinda sad it's all over."

He put his hand in hers and hugged it tightly. "You shouldn't be, Mom," he said. "We will come there again. You and I and Eric, will come there again. Maybe next year…"

She didn't answer, and the boy looked at her face. "We will, won't we?" he asked worriedly.

"Yes, Anders, we probably will, maybe next year…or the next."

She knew he had no real concept of time, and she couldn't bear to explain everything to him. She didn't want to speak. Just sit there in silence while the boat slowly made its way over the sun-glittering waters with a tail in its wake.

"I think Eric is just like Dad. He's kind and fun. Can't you ask if he wants to be my Dad, Mom?"

Lise flinched and went completely numb. She had never guessed that the boy harbored such thoughts. She had almost begun to think that he had forgotten about Michael. But this…

She looked at him, almost horrified, and hoped that Eric had not heard this. "You … you must never say things like that, Anders. Not so Eric hears it. Never!"

"But why not? You also like him."

"Yes, Anders, I like him too." She hugged the boy close to her. "I like him very much, but he can never be your father, my boy."

"Why not?" Anders asked.

"Because…because he might have some other…" Lise whispered.

She didn't know if she was telling the truth or lying.

She knew nothing about the tall, dark man standing by the helm and staring out over the water.

Nothing more than that his name was Eric Roy and that she loved him with all her heart.

The motorboat settled carefully at the mooring by the pier. Eric helped her and Anders ashore, and they walked up the promenade while Cameron stayed behind to tinker the boat.

Lise suddenly felt tired. She would soon stand face to face with Beth again. She would be forced to explain in minute detail what they had done, and the mere thought of it sickened her to the stomach.

She heard someone call a name, and she felt how Eric stiffened. He slowly turned his head, and Lise saw a young girl with long blond hair waving at him.

Once again, she called a name, and Eric looked as if punched in the groin, and he turned quickly to Lise.

"I must leave you," he said with a hoarse voice. "There is someone I need to speak to. Can you manage by yourself?"

"Of course," Lise replied. "Just go."

He nodded. His eyes were sad and confused, his gaze filled with fear, and she didn't understand why.

He quickly bent down and kissed Anders on the forehead, then he turned and walked into the park towards the beautiful blond woman who called for him.

Lise did not stop to observe their meeting. Instead, she took Anders's hand and continued.

Her thoughts were a mess. She pondered the name the woman had called out.

It hadn't been Eric.

She has heard it clearly. And she had seen how distraught Eric had become.

The name the girl had called was, "Pierre!"

"Pierre, what are you doing in this neck of the woods?

The young blond woman smiled, but there was confusion in her eyes, and she looked like she regretted calling for him. His initial fear had turned into something resembling anger. Why was she here? He wondered if Lise had caught the name that she called.

"I could ask you the same," he commented stiffly. He glanced around the park. She seemed to be alone. She had obviously been heading toward one of the hotels when she'd seen him in the company with Lise and Anders.

"Oh, me?" Clara shrugged. "I'm on a little tour with Bob Hutchinson from New York. I don't think you know him. He is a very successful businessman. We…we got engaged last week," she added uncertainly.

Pierre looked at her. She was still gorgeous, but he no longer understood what he had seen in her. There was something cold and spoiled about her that Lise completely lacked. Lise was warm, alive, and human, whereas Clara seemed empty, hard, and clueless.

"Congratulations," he said. "I … I wish you all the happiness in the world, Clara."

"Shall we sit?" she said. "I don't have much time. Bob is in town to fix something. We'll continue west later today and all the way to Vancouver. He has some business interests there."

They settled down on a park bench. Her face was tanned and healthy, and she actually looked younger than he remembered.

"Sounds like a serious trip," he said, just to say something.

"We flew from New York yesterday. Bob is an experienced pilot and has a lovely little Cirrus jet to fly us in."

She suddenly fell silent and took his hand.

"But you still haven't explained what you're doing here, Pierre?"

"Have you forgotten that I am on the run from the law?" he said dryly.

"No, I haven't forgotten that. And I totally checked when I saw you. Everyone thinks you fled to Mexico and South America."

Then I was right, he thought. The police had picked up his false trace of the tickets he purchased for Texas and never thought he'd go north.

"Why did you do it, Pierre?" Her voice was low and accusing, but she kept his hand in hers.

"What do you mean?" His words snapped.

"Why didn't you stay and take your punishment? It would have been over in a breeze, and then..."

She fell silent when she saw the shadows of fury in his eyes. She remembered his face well; that nerve by his eye that bulged when he got upset, the dark anger in his gaze.

"Would you have done it?" he exclaimed fiercely. "Would you have stayed and let them lock you up in a cell for a crime you didn't commit?"

He withdrew his hand and ran his fingers through his thick dark hair.

"But, Pierre, it was only six months. And six months pass so fast. Many people have been in prison for six months and come out for a new start as if nothing happened."

As if nothing had happened… He stared at her. She was as clueless as a child. She couldn't empathize with other people's feelings and thoughts; she would never understand what being confined meant to him. She was a beautiful and spoiled child; life was nothing but a game. It was no use to try and explain this to her. She wouldn't understand.

"I just couldn't, Clara," he said wearily. "My nerves were a mess, and I just had to get away from everything."

"I was terribly disappointed," she said. "I had not expected this from you. You were a man, after all."

He did not reply. There was no point. She would never understand the terrible panic that seized him when the prosecutor called and said he would go to prison the following day.

They sat in silence. She studied his face, and suddenly she was filled with compassion. This was something new to her. Before, she had only felt contempt for his selfish action, but now she noted how thin he had become, how tender and tense and sad his face looked. He seemed to have aged many years.

"Shouldn't you go back, Pierre?" she asked softly. "For your own sake. You can't go on living on the run. There is no future."

"Being on the run is hell, Clara!" He shook his head. "But I can't go back. I cannot surrender myself to a corrupt system. And I have probably already burned all bridges."

"By the way, have you heard anything?" he said after a moment of silence. It was an unnecessary question. If she had any news, she would have told him already.

"No," she said. "I quit the job at the Department of Justice after your trial. I couldn't stand everyone staring at me and whispering behind me. I… I had to leave D.C., and Dad helped me with an apartment in Manhattan. He thought it was the best way for a new start."

Well, thought Pierre bitterly, *the powerful Eric G. Busch thought it best that his daughter broke all ties with the past.*

"But I know your case was scheduled for the Attorney General," Clara continued. "He had received it just before I quit, but… Do you really think you have a chance? I mean, both instances were in agreement."

"No," he said softly, "deep down, I don't think I have a chance. But oddly enough, hope is all that remains."

They sat in silence. They had nothing more to tell each other. What had once been between them was finally gone. It should never have been.

Clara looked at the clock, then she got up.

"Good heavens, it's late. Bob is probably waiting for me at the hotel. I have to rush."

Pierre also stood. They looked at each other for a moment, then she tiptoed and kissed him lightly.

"God be with you, Pierre," she whispered. "It was sad it had to turn the way it did, but we were never really meant for each other. I hope that…that you somehow get out of this," she added, turned, and hurried out of the park.

He stayed and watched her slim back disappear, then he shrugged and strolled in the opposite direction.

Clara had killed the last remains of hope he had harbored.

He was still hunted.

He would always be hunted.

As he walked, he wondered what Lise was thinking right now. Had Clara raised suspicions in her?

He could send her a text, but a visit was better. He owed her that much. Tomorrow he would go to her and thank her for their time.

Then he would leave Neuveville forever.

Beth was sitting in her rocking chair on the porch when Lise and Anders came home. She returned their greeting briefly, and when Anders ran up to her with a kiss, she let it happen without any enthusiasm.

Lise felt that there was thunder in the air. Beth was probably furious that she had left for the hike. She didn't ask how they'd been and if they had a good time.

"We will eat in half an hour," she stated shortly. "Maybe you'd better go and get ready. You look like you need a bath, but you mustn't let Anders wet the whole bathroom. Ana cleaned everything while you were gone."

She continued her knitting to indicate that she was done with them—for the time being.

While bathing the boy, she wondered why the strange woman in the park had called Eric Pierre. Eric had also immediately reacted to the name.

I must not mistrust him, she thought as she scrubbed Anders, making him howl in annoyance and delight. *Eric doesn't owe me any explanations, and I have no demands on him.*

And yet she knew this was not true. When you love, you want to know everything about that person; and she loved Eric. She no longer tried to hide the fact from herself. During the last few days, they had become very close, even though they still did not know much about each other. The mere thought that she wouldn't see more of him filled her with despair and loneliness that almost hurt.

Why did he always pull away from her?

By now, he must know how she felt about him. He was a man with a man's understanding, yet he drew away as soon as she happened to touch him.

Why?

When they were clean, they went down to eat. Only Anders spoke, oblivious to the hostile silence that his grandmother exuded.

"And I'm a trapper now, Grandma," he said. "I'm a real trapper. Ranger Tom taught me how to trap rats and when—"

Beth pressed her lips together. "I'm not having a trapper under my roof," she said. "To me, you are Anders, my grandson, and that is what you'll remain."

The boy blushed and looked at his mum. She shook her head, and he finished his meal in utter silence. As he left the table, he did not say thanks for the food, and Lise had to call him back to give his grandmother a kiss. He obeyed with a visible protest.

"I'll put him to bed," said Lise and got up. "He is tired and needs to sleep."

"Come back after that," said Beth. "I want to talk to you."

Lise had to sit a long time on the edge of Anders's bed for him to calm down.

"Why was Grandma so angry?" he asked. "And why did she say that about the trappers?"

"Grandma is old," replied Lise, stroking him gently on the cheek. "She has other values than us."

The boy nodded, and his eyes were big and cloudy from fatigue. "I don't think she is mad with the trappers. I think it is for Eric."

"Eric?" Lise looked on in surprise. How could he know what the old woman was thinking?

"Yes, she doesn't like him. One evening before we left for the hike, she told me I should never forget my father. There was no one in the whole world like my dad. I never should forget him."

No, Lise thought bitterly. *No one in the world was like your father. He lied to me, cheated on me, and I would have left him if that accident had not happened. There was no one like him…*

When she left to go downstairs to her mother-in-law, she felt uneasy. She hated having to answer before Beth and feared what she might say if she lost control. Beth knew nothing about what happened between Michael and her, nor did she want to tell.

Depriving someone of their illusions wasn't the best thing to do. Most of the time, it was unnecessary, merciless, and cruel. Just pointless.

Beth sat outside in the rocking chair again. The evening was warm, and the roses smelled heavenly.

"You wanted to talk to me," Lise said, sitting on the bench along the porch railing. The twilight turned the air blue, and silhouettes of birds circled against the rose-colored clouds towards the mountains in the north. Up there, she had been free, the smell of wood and log fires in the cabin, Eric's tormented nightmare, and how she calmed him with a kiss he wasn't aware of.

What was he doing right now?

And why had that strange woman called him Pierre?

"What do you know about that man?" Beth's voice snapped her out of her thoughts, and she blushed slightly.

It was as if the old woman had read her thoughts.

"What man?" she said to buy time.

"Don't act more stupid than you are, Lise." Beth's voice was harsh and hostile; she had let the knitting rest. "You know that I'm talking about that man who dragged you to the forest. Do you know that he is an imposter?"

Lise froze. For a moment, she was filled with wild anxiety. What did Beth know? What did she intend to reveal?

"He is no impostor," she answered calmly. "Whatever gave you that idea? He has given Anders and me an unforgettable experience. I am very grateful to him."

"And what did you give him in return?" her mother-in-law said mockingly.

They looked at each other, and Beth had to look away in the end.

"Well, anyway," she muttered. "He is not who he pretends to be. You must understand that I only want what's best for you."

"I don't understand anything," answered Lise sharply. "I won't sit here and listen to an old woman's dirty thoughts." She rose, but Beth's next words made her ice cold.

"Not even if the old woman found out something about that man you want to see so eagerly?"

"What do you mean?" Her heart filled with worry.

"Doctor Aubert came here and examined me right after you left," Beth continued softly. "He had something quite interesting to say about your Mr. Roy. He had cared for him during his recent illness, and despite Mr. Roy's declaration to his hosts that he is an engineer, Dr. Aubert has a strong feeling that his patient has a medical degree."

A medical degree? Lise closed her eyes. She found support against the porch railing. Suddenly she remembered how professionally Eric had examined the sick woman and how calmly and confidently he established a diagnosis.

"I don't think so," she whispered.

"You can believe what you want," said Beth, "but that's what Dr. Aubert told me; he usually has sharp eyes."

"Mr. Roy is an engineer from Washington D.C."

"How do you know for sure? Has he shown you his papers?"

"He doesn't have to show me any papers!" Lise snapped fiercely. "I'm not going to listen to more of your insidious insinuations. You just are jealous because I found a friend, because Anders found a male role model who deals with him and can make him forget all the horrible things he has experienced."

"But you must be forgetting that I also have a responsibility for the boy! He is my grandson. And there is a clause in Canadian law that states that a child can be taken from their mother and given to a father or grandmother if the mother is unable to care for them properly."

Lise stared at the old woman. At first, she thought that she had heard wrong. But then she saw that the mother-in-law's eyes were filled with seriousness.

"You…you're disgusting," she whispered. "I don't think you meant what you just said."

"I have consulted with my lawyer," replied Beth.

"I…I can't…" Lise turned away. For a moment, she had a strong desire to tell everything about Michael, about his lies, his infidelity, his drinking, his brutality.

But she couldn't. The old woman had such narrow horizons that she would never understand, let alone believe her.

"We are leaving," she said. "I'll stay for a few days, not to worry Anders, but then we leave. And no lawyer in the world will be able to stop us," she added. "Anders is my son, and you"—she turned and stared at the old woman with resentment—"you have lost all rights to him. Good night."

Pierre hesitated outside the gate. It was ten o'clock, and he could see the old woman, Lise's mother-in-law, sitting in her rocking chair on the porch.

The morning was full of sunshine and warmth, but when he got up at seven o'clock, there had been a thin layer of ice on the water barrel below his window.

He opened the gate and went up the garden path.

"Good morning," he said. "I'm Eric Roy. I'd like to speak with Lise—with Mrs. Norrgard?"

The old woman glared at him with hostility.

"She is not at home," she snarled. "She's out."

"And Anders?

"He is with her."

Pierre stood confused for a moment, then he shrugged his shoulders and turned to leave.

"You don't have to come back," she cried after him. "We don't want you here. Lise wants no more of you."

He stopped. Her words had hit him like whiplash, and slowly, he turned to face her. "I don't understand."

"Oh, you sure do. My daughter-in-law doesn't want to be with a man who is an imposter. Just you leave her alone."

Pierre nodded.

"I... I am sorry," he murmured.

He continued to the gate as if in a fog. Lise must have found out who he was. And now she no longer wanted to see him.

He walked along the sidewalk of Rue du Pont. People brushed against him, but he barely noticed.

At the promenade, he turned west. He had no bathing trunks and had no real intention of going to the beach, but now he felt a strong need to be alone.

He had wanted to see Lise.

He had been awake most of the night, and when he finally fell asleep, he was determined to seek her out and tell her everything.

He could no longer remain silent.

He loved her. He had become addicted to her and the boy. He couldn't leave them without telling her the truth. And if she still wanted him after that, he had decided to return to Washington D.C. and take his sentence.

But fate had gotten ahead of him.

Lise had found out who he was, and now she had made it clear that she didn't want anything to do with him.

It had to be, he thought. Maybe it was for the best.

But inside, he felt an emptiness and despair that no logic could erase. It was as if the sunny summer day had suddenly turned into a cold and withering autumn day with dead leaves on the branches, yellow grass on the ground, and frost in the sand.

He was about fifty paces from their usual place when he caught sight of them.

Lise sat by the rock, her back resting on the warm stone, and Anders climbed high up in a tree.

She got up immediately, smiling brightly at him, and ran toward him, throwing herself around his neck, and pressed her lips against his.

"Oh, Eric," she whispered. "I didn't think you would come. I have been waiting. I have been worried. But you came."

For a moment, he stood silently with his arms around her. He felt her young firm body against his, and he was filled with intense happiness.

She had been waiting for him.

She was here, pressed close to him. She loved him…

"Eric! Eric!" The boy in the tree gave up a shout of joy. "Look, Eric! Look at me when I climb down!"

At that moment, it happened. In his eagerness to climb down swiftly, the boy lost his grip on the branch and fell backward, the small hands desperately clutching for something to hold on to. He fell headlong to the ground.

Pierre rushed to him. He fell to his knees next to the small motionless body that had been so full of life and joy seconds before.

The boy lay with his eyes closed. He breathed faintly, and his pulse fluttered.

"Oh, Eric!" Lise was on her knees beside him. She motioned to lift Anders's head to her lap, but Pierre stopped her. He lifted one eyelid, then let it go.

Pierre felt his stomach drop as he looked down at the boy. He could see the jagged edges of a large rock protruding from beneath the boy's head. He could taste the fear in his throat.

Anders must have hit his skull on the rock when he fell. He was unconscious, his limp tiny frame was motionless, and a deep gash in his head bled profusely onto the sand, revealing the white gleam of bone beneath.

"Eric…what is it? Is…is he badly injured?" Lise's voice was tinged with despair, but when she reached out to pick up her boy, he stopped her again.

"Don't touch him," he said sharply. "We must call for an ambulance, Lise."

There was an authority in his voice that she had heard once before when he examined the sick woman in the camp.

Pierre dialed the emergency services and instructed them to immediately send an ambulance.

Lise looked at him, frightened but also confused about the precise orders he conveyed to the person over the phone.

"Go and meet them, Lise. Show them the way, and I'll stay here with Anders."

For a moment, they looked at each other, then she nodded. He remained on his knees next to the boy.

His lips felt dry, and he wished it wouldn't take long. It was a matter of minutes, never hours.

He recognized the symptoms all too well, and yet he couldn't believe it.

The boy was dying.

The ambulance rushed down the Promenade with wailing sirens.

Lise sat beside her boy, and Pierre sat on a bench behind the driver. They hadn't exchanged many words since the paramedics arrived and, on Pierre's command, gently lifted Anders on the stretcher and brought him into the ambulance.

Lise hadn't cried, and Pierre was grateful for it. Time was short, and hysterical tears would hardly improve the situation.

But she hadn't spoken either. Instinctively, she had understood that her son's condition was severe. Still, she didn't ask a lot of unnecessary questions. But her large beautiful eyes were dark with sorrow and worry, and she had a worried expression around her mouth. Every now and then, she bit her lip as if to hold back her tears.

The hospital was located a short distance outside Neuveville on a height overlooking Lake Sables. The maples in the park had already started to turn yellow, but the flower beds along the black driveway flaunted enormous yellow roses with splashes of red in them. *Roses of peace,* Pierre thought. *Peace…*

Two nurses received them at the ER entrance. He quickly and automatically explained to them how important it was that the boy was moved with the greatest care. They nodded. One of them—a stout blonde who made him think of sister Elena in D.C.— raised an eyebrow and asked, "Are you a medical doctor?"

He didn't answer but turned and put his arm around Lise's shoulders as they followed the gurney into the hospital.

He knew it wasn't a big hospital, but he also knew these smaller regional places often had good equipment and modern operating rooms with all conceivable technical aids. He just hoped there was a skilled surgeon on the payroll.

The nurses disappeared with the gurney into an operation room, and soon after, a doctor came rushing. She was quite young, with lively eyes and scruffy hair. She looked like she had just woken up from a nap, but her handshake was firm as she introduced herself.

"I'm Dr. Caroline."

"The boy must be X-rayed immediately," said Pierre.

"Of course," the doctor replied, a little surprised. "What has happened?"

Pierre spoke quickly and concisely about the accident, and the young doctor's face grew serious. She glanced at Lise. "Is that the boy's mother?"

Pierre nodded.

"We'll see what we can do," the doctor mumbled, disappearing into the operating room.

Pierre and Lise sat down on a bench. She said nothing, but she took his hand and clutched it tightly.

A moment later, the doctor returned.

"The boy is being X-rayed," she said softly to Pierre. "We will get the results at any time. I hope…"

"I would like to take a look at them," Pierre interrupted.

Doctor Caroline looked at him in surprise. She was about to say something, but then she stopped herself.

She didn't understand what a layman could make out from a couple of X-rays.

"Perhaps you should contact Quebec in the meantime," Pierre suggested. "If you don't feel confident doing the surgery yourself?"

Once again, the young doctor looked surprised. But then she smiled a little pale smile.

"You are right," she said. "I'm not a neurosurgeon, and this could be complicated."

"They can send a skilled surgeon from Quebec. He or she can be here in just a few hours."

Doctor Caroline did not answer. A nurse came through the corridor and announced that the X-ray was finished.

Pierre followed Doctor Caroline to the large screen displaying the boy's head. The young doctor studied the images, and her face grew a shade paler.

Without a word, she looked at Pierre, then asked the nurse:

"Call Quebec right away. No, by the way, I'll call myself ..."

She nodded to Pierre and disappeared into a room. They heard her voice but could not make out the words, just that she sounded excited.

Pierre studied the X-rays and felt sweat break out at his hairline.

It was worse than he feared.

Splinters from the skull had penetrated the cerebral cortex in several places and caused bleeding. It was impossible to determine how far it had penetrated without surgery.

Anders should be operated on immediately; every second was precious.

He looked at Lise and saw her desperation, and his mouth was as dry as the desert.

If he explained who he was, the boy would have a chance. It was a slim chance, but it was.

But if he came forward, that would be the end of himself. He had no doubt that the hospital staff would consider it their duty to contact the police.

Doctor Caroline returned. Her young face could not hide what she had learned. She looked at Pierre.

”The hospital in Quebec did not have a surgeon available right now, but someone could be here in three hours.”

She gave Lise a look. But Lise looked out the window as if unaware of what was happening around her.

”And that would be too late,” added Dr. Caroline with a low voice.

”I know.” Pierre's voice was impersonal.

The doctor looked at him in confusion.

”I ... I don't know what to do. I could, of course, attempt it myself, but I am not experienced in surgery like this. It requires a specialist, and even then…” She shrugged.

”So, you don't think there is a chance?”

They both flinched. Lise had risen and quietly approached them. She stared at the young Doctor, her deep sorrow written on her face like an open book. Lise's despair seemed to reach out of her, her heart pounding and her breath catching in her throat, enveloping them in a blanket of grief.

Pierre looked at her and felt heavy as lead, and he did not know what to do.

Doctor Caroline shook her head.

"I'm sorry, Mrs. Norrgard. But this is a case for a specialist, and unfortunately—"

"Get ready for surgery!"

The words came so unexpectedly and distinctly that it felt like someone had thrown a stone through a pane of glass.

Lise and Caroline looked at Pierre in astonishment, and only then did he understand that the words came from him.

"What…what do you mean?" said Dr. Caroline. "By what right can you—a layman—come here and—"

"Get ready for surgery," Pierre repeated calmly. "I'm taking over the case."

Lise's pupils dilated, and the young Doctor's face turned red with frustration.

"Who are you then?" she said a little ironically.

"I am Pierre Lyon-Cote. Doctor Pierre Lyon-Cote from Saint Orbona Hospital in Washington, D.C., and I am a specialist in cases like this. You may have heard my name, Doctor Caroline?"

"Doctor Lyon-Cote? Pierre Lyon-Cote from Washington D.C....yes, yes, of course," Caroline stammered. "Of course I have. But—"

"Doctor Caroline," said Pierre patiently. "I have no time for detailed explanations."

He no longer cared that there were nurses in the corridor who listened to him. He didn't care that Lise's face now was as confused as it was worried. He just knew he had to operate.

There was no other way if Anders was going to have a chance of survival.

"I am wanted by the police," he continued. "I am staying in Neuveville under a false name. But I can assure you that I am Pierre Lyon-Cote, and as the situation demands, I have decided to operate on the boy."

Doctor Caroline's face was motionless, her thoughts no longer possible to read. But then, she smiled and bowed slightly.

"Can I assist Dr. Lyon-Cote?" she said. "It would be a great honor."

"Of course."

While Caroline was giving orders to the nurses, Pierre turned to Lise. She stood motionless, and her hands were ice cold when he took them.

"And who are you?" she whispered.

"You heard that, right?"

She nodded, and her eyes filled up with tears.

"Yes, Eric—yes, Pierre—I heard that. And whatever happens, I will stand by your side. I don't understand, but I don't think you could have done anything bad." Her lips trembled. "Go to Anders. Take care of him for me…for us. And, God be with you," she added softly, holding his hands as tightly as if she would never let him go.

The surgery lasted three hours.

Pierre worked methodically and with all his skill. His hands were perfectly at ease, and he was barely aware that the little boy lying on the operating table was Anders, the boy who clung to his neck and once asked him if he couldn't be his father. Everything he had learned in the past was suddenly back in the present, and he worked with all his knowledge and his experience at the operating theater.

Only when the nurse wiped his forehead with a cool napkin did he notice how intensely he worked.

He had removed the last splinter of bone, and he felt that the operation was complete. There was nothing more he could do. All they could do now was hope everything would turn out well.

He straightened up. He ordered the nurse to suck up some blood that seeped out from under the skull bone. A few minutes later, he watched another nurse quickly and skillfully put a bandage around the boy's shaved head.

Doctor Caroline came up to him.

"That was fantastic, Doctor Lyon-Cote," she said, looking at Pierre with evident admiration.

"You were quite fantastic yourself, Doctor Caroline," smiled Pierre. "Without your assistance, it would have been significantly more difficult."

He hesitated momentarily and looked at the boy who lay with his eyes closed as the nurses rolled his bed to recovery.

"Would...would you please be so kind as to tell his mother everything went well. If nothing unexpected happens, her little boy will recover pretty soon."

Doctor Caroline shook her head. "No, Doctor Lyon-Cote, I cannot do that."

Pierre looked at her in surprise.

"You will have to do that yourself, Doctor Lyon-Cote," the younger Doctor hastened to say. "The boy would not live if it wasn't for your experience. You should break the news to his mother."

Pierre stood still for a moment, then he nodded.

"All right," he muttered. "I'll do it then."

"And Doctor Lyon-Cote…" Caroline looked at him with a smile. "You mentioned something about being involved with authorities. I don't know what it's about, but you can rest assured that no one at this hospital will interfere in your private affairs. We are full of admiration and appreciation for what you have just done, and as far as I am concerned, that is the only thing that matters. Good luck."

"Thank you, Dr. Caroline," Pierre murmured. "Thanks."

He took plenty of time to get changed. He wished someone would bring him a glass of whisky. His hands were trembling, and he was suddenly aware that he was facing something final.

When he came out into the waiting room, Lise stood up slowly. She looked worriedly at him, and he said softly, "There is nothing to worry about, Lise. The operation went well, and Anders will live. He's strong, the summer has made wonders with his physique and mental strength, and I hardly believe we need to fear any complications."

"You?" she said, looking wide-eyed at him.

He shook his head. "No, not me, Lise. I'm just a mechanic. It was a combination of fortunate circumstances."

Then she was in his arms, crying, but he couldn't see her face. She had buried it in his shoulder.

"Can…can I see him?" she sobbed. "Can I go to him?"

"By all means," he replied. "But it will be a while until he wakes up. And it is not certain that he recognizes you immediately."

They stood close to each other, and the touch of her body against his hurt. He slowly pushed her away.

"I must leave you now, Lise," he said. "I must go."

"Go?" She stared at him in dismay. "Where?"

"I have made my decision. I can't go on being on the run. I must surrender to the police."

Her lips moved without forming any words. She held out her hand as if to stop him from leaving. She looked up the corridor that led into the hospital. Then she quickly turned back to him.

"I'm coming with you," she said calmly. "Anders doesn't need me until later. Right now, you have a greater need for me."

She came up to him and took his hand, and they left the hospital together.

When they came out into the sunshine, she said:

"Whatever you've done, Pierre, I'll wait for you. Anders and I will be there for you when you come out from the prison."

All his uncertainty was suddenly wiped away, and he knew what he was about to do was the only right thing.

He should have done it a long time ago. It would have spared him the last months' anxiety and emotional turmoil.

The police station was on a street corner on Rue du Pont.

When they entered, a young constable stood at the counter looking at his cell phone. He looked up, uninterested. Pierre recognized him. It was the same policeman who had been watching the bus station the evening they came to Neuveville.

But Pierre was no longer frightened by the sight of the policeman.

"Can I speak to the supervisor on duty?" he asked.

"What is it about?"

"A report."

"A report? I can take that, " said the policeman, tapping on the computer keyboard.

"I don't think so," said Pierre. "I want to report myself. I would be grateful if I could speak to the chief constable."

A bit of excitement suddenly sparked in the young policeman's eyes. He turned and walked into a room inside behind the counter. After a few seconds, he returned, followed by an older man without the uniform jacket. The man looked curiously at Pierre and Lise.

"You wanted to report yourself," he said. "For what?"

"My name is Pierre Lyon-Cote," Pierre said. "Doctor Pierre Lyon-Cote from Washington D.C. I am wanted in the U.S. Maybe you are aware of that?"

The chief constable shook his head.

"Not that I remember, doctor, should I?"

"Nearly three months ago, I accidentally hit and killed a pedestrian while driving to an emergency on the highway in D.C.," Pierre said calmly. "I was brought before the court. The judge sentenced me to one year in prison and twenty-five thousand dollars in fines. Of the prison sentence, six months would be considered conditional. The conviction was appealed, but the higher court found no reason to change it. The day before I was supposed to go to prison, I escaped. I traveled here, to Neuveville, under the false name of Eric Roy. This is where I have hidden over the last few months. But now, I have decided to turn myself in."

The chief constable scratched the back of his neck.

"Lyon-Cote…Pierre Lyon-Cote…I may have read something about that. Jonathan…" He turned to the young constable. "Can you see if there are any warrants on Dr. Lyon-Cote?"

The constable started tapping on the keyboard.

Jonathan, thought Pierre. *Jonathan White.* That was the name of the policeman who came to visit the Camerons and had scared the crap out of Pierre. And all he wanted was to ask old Bernard if he could play in the police brass band.

He smiled tiredly and felt Lise squeeze his hand.

All that felt so far away. It was like it all occurred in another existence, another world. He had now returned to reality, and the only thing that mattered was that he came to his senses. And he was well on the way. He no longer feared the thought of a prison cell. The isolation did not scare him. For he was not alone.

He looked at Lise and smiled again.

"You must go back to Anders later," he said.

She nodded.

"Yes. But we'll come back. To you," she whispered.

Constable White looked up, turned to his superior, and pointed to the screen. The chief constable pushed down the glasses parked on the forehead and started reading. Now and then nodded to himself.

When he finished, he turned his face to meet Pierre's eyes.

"Sorry, Doctor Lyon-Cote…but we don't want you anymore." He smiled. "If we had known about you a month ago, I would gladly have locked you up for transfer to the Americans, but it is no longer needed."

Pierre stared at him questioningly.

"There was a new message from Washington D.C. just a week ago. Apparently, the Attorney General has dismissed your conviction. You only have to pay one thousand dollars for administrative charges, and you're a free man."

A free man!

Pierre's hands clutched the counter. He heard Lise heave a deep sigh of relief—or was it he? Then the chief constable straightened his back, put the glasses up his reclining hairline, and said, "Good luck, Dr. Lyon-Cote. The hunt is over, and the game seemed to have escaped unhurt." He laughed.

His laughter followed them out into the street.

The game escaped unhurt, thought Pierre. *I'm not so sure,* looking at the woman beside him. *Is it really so?*

"Come," she said, tucking her arm under his. "Come on, Pierre. There is nothing more to fear. We're going to Anders. He will be overjoyed when he wakes up and sees us. I must also call my mother-in-law and tell her everything. And then ..."

She fell silent.

She stood still and looked at him. A slight blush colored her cheeks; she had never been more beautiful.

People passed them on the street, staring at them, but he didn't care.

He had a complete disregard for what people thought.

"I owe you something," he said.

"Owe me?" Her green eyes were wide.

"Yes," he said, "it is something I ought to have done long ago."

And she never got the chance for more questions because how can a woman ask when she is locked in an iron-tight grip, and her lips are pressed passionately in a kiss that never wanted to end?

People stared at them.

People nudged each other in the side and smiled.

But the warm summer breeze had been replaced by the cooler wind from the north—a wind which announced that the short summer was soon being replaced by fall.

And they ignored it all.

The summer at Lake Sables was coming to a close, but the promise of fresh beginnings filled their hearts with love and warmth.

Yesteryear's stories reflected today
Yabot AB
www.yabot.se

www.ingramcontent.com/pod-product-compliance
Lightning Source LLC
LaVergne TN
LVHW041318200726

843509LV00009B/536